ALSO FROM EX-CATHEDRA

Voices from the Cathedral (2010)

Ten Minute Tales (2017)

TALES FOR OUR TIMES

An anthology of stories written and collected by members of
Ex-Cathedra, a Norwich-based writing group,

Shirley Buxton

Alison Court

Patrick Linehan

Stuart McCarthy

Moira Newlan

Avril Suddaby

Nicola L C Talbot

Published by Smokehouse Press, Norwich

First published in 2024
by Smokehouse Press
Norwich, NR1 4HB
www.smokehousepress.co.uk

Typeset in Cambria by Smokehouse Press
Printed and bound by CMP (uk) Ltd.

Cover photographs © Ken Newlan
@kennewlan

ISBN 978-9152832-20

*This book is dedicated to the memory of
Graham Porter, who was instrumental in forming the Ex-
Cathedra Writing Group, keeping the show on the road always
encouraging us to believe in ourselves as writers*

CONTENTS

FOREWORD FROM SAINT MARTINS HOUSING TRUST

At St Martins we know that every person has a unique story; some of the people we support have suffered unimaginable trauma and are often in the depths of despair, some just need a helping hand, specialist support or a listening ear. We support people when they are at their most vulnerable, often encouraging them into accommodation when they have been sleeping rough on the streets of Norwich.

We support people out of homelessness and into independence, helping them focus on the lives they want to lead. We support people to know that there is a better future for them.

Over my time as Chief Executive of St Martins, a homelessness charity based in Norwich, I have met hundreds of people who have lived in our residential settings, in the community, and on the streets of Norwich. Whilst no two experiences are the same, sometimes there are similar threads that unite their stories; loss, trauma, broken relationships and poverty. There are also tremendous examples of resilience, tenacity, kindness and hope.

Some of these themes are addressed in *Tales for Our Times*, this makes this book a powerful and informative read, recognising not only the fragility of life and the difficult situations that some people have to deal with, but also the strength of human spirit and the kindness of strangers.

We find a sense of 'home' not only in the four walls around us and the roof over our heads, but in our community, our culture, the memories that ground us, and the people that we live with. At

St Martins we always say there is more to homelessness than housing.

It is an enormous privilege to be asked to write the foreword for this book and for St Martins to benefit from charitable donations from the sale of *Tales for Our Times*. My colleagues and I enjoy speaking to groups about the work of St Martins and we had the privilege of meeting some of the Ex-Cathedra group.

St Martins was granted Freedom of the City in 2022 and is embedded into the story of Norwich – the charity started its life in the garage of the Dean of the Cathedral. Over the last 50 years we've grown to meet the needs of local people, offering many different types of accommodation from emergency services to hostels, from residential care to sheltered housing – one size certainly doesn't fit all when we are supporting people. Now, at any one-time St Martins supports over 300 people with an incredible 200 team members.

We can only do the work we do with the support and understanding of local people. Helping people to understand why some people become homeless or sleep rough is an important part of our work. This incredible book will help and support us to spread awareness about homelessness, rough sleeping and our life saving work.

I am grateful to the Ex-Cathedra group for tackling the complex issues related to our work and supporting us to raise awareness and funds.

Dr Jan Sheldon

Chief Executive, St Martins

Introduction from a member of Ex-Cathedra

It was after a visit to a meeting of the Ex-Cathedra writers' group, by a speaker from St Martin's Housing Trust, that I volunteered to participate in their December street collection. I had never done anything like that before and had my doubts about how effective a method of fundraising it could be.

December was, on the whole, a depressing month with rain at least every other day. I was lucky, and the day I reported for duty was cold, but not wet. After being given a tabard to identify me as a certified collector, and a collecting tin, I set off for central Norwich.

At first, I stood, rather self-consciously in front of Waterstones. I was to be disappointed in the response from the reading and present buying people entering and leaving the store; most of them just looked through me as if I didn't exist. This was proving to be a waste of time, so I decided to use a more direct approach. Settling on potential donors, I would ask, "Would you give a contribution to the St Martin's Trust for the homeless?" or, "Please would you help the homeless?" or some similar variation, while offering my collecting tin. A few people gave, but most said, "No thanks," or "Not now."

This was not going well and my hands and feet were getting very cold. I moved on to Jarrolds corner and decided not to approach anyone but instead to rattle my tin of coins and make as much noise as possible. This was a far more effective approach. Most people looked to see what the noise was, and I was soon encouraged by the steady flow of donations, many of them extremely generous. It may be a generalisation to say that older people gave more readily than younger ones, or that those who looked least affluent often surprised me by giving notes rather than coins, but it sometimes did seem to be the case. Several donors stopped to chat, and to ask about St Martin's and to give their opinions about the problem of homelessness. The only bad language I heard was directed at the politicians who so signally failed to address the issue.

There were a few particularly interesting encounters. One man told me that in his opinion I was wasting my time; he thought prayer was the answer and that God would solve our problems. Another man said he was in need of charity himself and tried to persuade me to hand over my collecting tin. I held on tightly to the tin and tried to explain that St Martin's was there to help many people, not just him. Eventually he moved away, none too pleased with my response.

What did I learn from such a stimulating if somewhat chilly morning? Well, street collections may not be the most effective way of raising money, but I was surprised to learn how much I had collected in my tin, and even more surprised to be told that, during the week, all the collectors, between them had raised £36,688.45.

And yes, I will do it again next year, and I will wear a silly hat to make myself more noticeable. I intend, in future, to be more generous myself when I'm invited to contribute to a street collection being carried out in a worthy cause. It will be notes that I give in future rather than just the £1 or £2 coins which I always used to think was enough. It's good to know that that these street collections are a benefit, not just to the St Martin's and their clients but to the collectors themselves without whose enthusiasm none of the money would be raised.

THE SILVER TOPS

Alison Court

Tooting Working Men's Club hadn't seen anything like it in more than twenty years, not since VE Day. Every house in the neighbourhood that owned a TV had hosted one of the numerous groups of four, five, ten, men, that now streamed in through the swinging doors, singing, chanting, swelling the heaving throng of happy red faces. The afternoon had seen many a pint quaffed — but after all, it was a once in a lifetime occasion.

Wedged in the window seat were four ample dinner ladies, white hair peeping out from under their cloche hats, bags on their knees. Edie, Maud, Bernadette and Renee had escaped their homes for the afternoon; they had gone to where there were, for just this once, no men — the Club. There they had wiled away a few happy hours over more than a few drinks, laughing and chatting and singing their favourite songs.

Now the room was noisier and ever more crowded, as the men who had had tickets for the match arrived back from Wembley. They called their orders to the bar over the heads of the men in front of them, and pint after pint was passed back to them. Not a drop was spilled, though the uproar might have knocked anyone off their stride.

Edie took another sip of her Babycham and leaned into her friends conspiratorially, "That Ernie," she bellowed, "he's had a few too many, if you ask me. Look at 'im," and she nodded over at the young man sagging over the bar.

"Engerlahnd!" chanted a voice out of the crowd, and the crowd chanted back. In the far corner of the room, where half a dozen men sat around the Irish table, you could just hear their riposte, "Wheesht, it's a wonder . . . ," and opposite them, where the Jamaicans played dominos, men pushed back their trilbies and huddled closer over their game. "Each unto his own," they said to each other. "Nice for them to have a win at last."

"Engerlahnd!" the crowd tunelessly carried on. The women looked at each other, waggled their hips comfortably up against one another and their eyes met. They each had the same idea at the same moment, but it was Bernadette, buoyed by her third half-pint of Guinness, who expressed it first.

"Come on gels, let's give 'em what for!!"

"Yeah, come on gels," Renee responded, standing up and raising her port and lemon. "Let's go for it!"

And, as one, the ample dinner ladies rose to their feet, raised their voices to the heavens and let rip, in four-part harmony, "Sugar Pie, Honey Bunch, I can't help myself".

The hubbub immediately next to them receded a little and a few of the men celebrating nearby turned to stare at the unusual sight and sound.

"When you snap your finger or wink your eye, I come a-running to you . . . " sang the ladies, and the hubbub receded further. By the time they reached, "When I call your name, Girl, it starts to flame," there was hush throughout the bar. Rowdy men had become putty in these aged ladies' hand - just like that.

The song drew to its end, there was a brief second's silence, and then, tumultuous applause.

"Blimey, gels, we fort we'd 'ad a good enough day before we even come in 'ere," said Len from number twenty-seven, "Nah yer givin' us a 'ole new show."

Maud knocked back the rest of her Cinzano, "C'mon, gels, nah the other one." And off they went again, breaking into, "I remember yet, before we met . . . "

A lone voice cut in, "Leave it out, will yer," and the crowd turned on him with a "Shusssh."

The ladies, gathering confidence in their audience, carried on, "Lovin' you has made my life so much sweeter than ever," and they waggled their hips again, a little, to show just how much they were moved by their song.

It drew to a close, as songs always must, and the ladies plumped themselves back down into their window seat and picked up their glasses. Singing was thirsty work.

"More, more!" yelled the crowd, stamping their feet in unison to show their appreciation.

Maud, Bernadette, Renee and Edie looked at each other. "We gotta get out, now," whispered Bernadette, before they find out we don't know no others. Leave 'em wantin' more, that's wot yer gotta do."

As one — again — they rose to their feet, their bags clutched before them. They inclined their heads to the throng, pushed the tables out of the way, and processed, with difficulty, towards the door. "More, more," they heard behind them, as they gained the warm summer's evening air outside.

"They fink it's all over," giggled Edie.

"Well, it is now," replied Bernadette, "but I'll tell yer what, we're goin' to do summat wiv this, we're goin' ter practise and we're goin' ter giv' 'em all a right ol' show."

The others stopped and looked at their friend agog. What a plan! They'd show everyone just what dinner ladies could do.

"Let's start now," said Renee, "let's go back ter mine and make a plan. Let's aim high!" And they set off down the street, the sounds of, "More, more!" behind them gradually wafting into, "Engerlahnd, Engerlahnd!"

And so it came to pass that the ladies had much to fill their hours after their working day was over. Over the next few months, they practised and practised the two songs they had performed that happy night in the Working Men's Club. For, if truth be told, they had not sung them perfectly that night, getting mixed up with the words in places, and sometimes the harmony hadn't quite worked out, though the audience, half cut as it was, was not an overcritical one. But by Guy Fawkes night, they knew their songs backwards and forwards and inside out.

"We gotta do a proper dance," they suddenly realised, and Maud, whose daughter had been to ballet lessons when she was little, said she would work out the steps and teach them.

"Blimey, I ain't never goin' to manage this," squealed Edie, as she tripped over yet again, but it's surprising what a difference it makes if you keep practicing, and soon they had a dance routine that would fare well against any competition from *Top of the Pops*.

Then one day Renee came flying in, "Dresses, gels, we gotta have proper dresses!"

Everyone turned to look at Bernadette. "Who? Me?" she said. For Bernadette had been a right good dressmaker when she was young and she still was adept with her flying needle. "That's a lotta work," she protested, "I ain't gonna make four fancy dresses all by meself. You're goin' ter have ter learn how to do it nexter me." She looked them each in the eye and they knew, it was going to be another learning curve — but what the . . . they'd learned so much already, why stop now?

The months passed. They were now kitted out with a basic repertoire, with the movements to go with it and with the dresses to perform in.

Come the end of July, and the first anniversary of that famous night down at the Working Men's Club, when England had at last won the World Cup, and the ladies were ready for their great concert at the Balham Hippodrome. The night was warm. The crowds were buoyant, and out to enjoy themselves. Our ladies had spent the morning at Doreen's Hairdressing Salon, down the High Road, and were pleased with the results, for their white waves had been given every treatment imaginable and looked almost silver atop their beaming faces. Backstage they donned their beautiful dresses, cut on the bias, which demonstrated the importance of good foundation wear. They were confident and happy. They knew it was going to go well.

Out on the stage, the host, in his crisp white jacket, his satin waistcoat and his golden bow tie, was stirring up the capacity crowd of family, friends and neighbours.

"Let me give you, ladies and gennelmen, the amazin', the wonderful, the gifted, the 'armonious, Silver Tops".

The crowd roared, as Maud, Edie, Renee and Bernadette shimmied onstage. "Mum, Mum, we love you," shouted several of their offspring, scattered throughout the stalls. The Silver Tops looked at each other across the deafening applause, Bernadette gave the beat, and off they set. One hit after another, every one meeting with a more rapturous response than the last.

At last, they were coming to the finale, and it was time for Renee to look Bernadette in the eye and sing the almighty *Bernadette*. "Bernadette, people are searchin' for The kind of love that we possessed ... "

The song came to a close, and Renee turned. The spotlight swept the stage and across the audience ... where, lo, an Afro-American gentleman, dressed in an immaculately fine ivory suit and bow-tie, with a neat moustache and deep, deep brown eyes, rose to his feet.

The eye of the audience alighted upon him; a collective sharp intake of breath. He swelled, he filled his lungs, he opened his mouth, and he sang, "Reach out ... " The audience exploded.

"Reach out . . . " The clamour raised the roof; the ladies reached out and pulled him up onto the stage. Yes, he was there.

Thus, the night ended, with Levi Stubbs, of the fabulous and famous Four Tops, singing alongside the Silver Tops.

Tooting and Balham had the best night they had ever had.

ONCE UPON A TIME

Avril Suddaby

"Once upon a time in America," the old story teller intoned, "herds of buffalo roamed the prairie which covered vast areas of this continent. This was before the white man arrived. The buffalo provided food and milk for us, skins for our clothing and for our teepees. There was more than enough for everyone. It was a generous land. Sometimes there were disputes, usually about encroachment onto the territories of another tribe, but such disputes were mostly settled without serious strife at the regular powwows, where our great leaders negotiated. Life was good for the Indians before the white man came to civilise us."

Despite the cataracts which made her almost totally blind, the storyteller knew that she was losing her audience. The old folk no longer paid attention; the young braves drifted away to drink themselves into a stupor at the reservation's liquor store. They had all heard too many times the story of how the settlers appropriated the tribal lands for their cattle, of how the buffalo were exterminated, of how the Indians were tricked into signing treaties which restricted them to the reservations on land which the settlers didn't want. Only the youngest children remained to listen to her. And they would soon grow up and join those who had lost the will to live as proud free men.

The story teller realised that she would have to find a new way to tell her story.

"Let us imagine," she said, "how life will be here in America in 500 years' time. How will the story go then?"

She began again, "Once upon a time in America, they will say, we Americans were the most advanced nation in the world. Our ideals and our faith gave us the courage and authority to act as the world's policeman. Our technology was superior, enabling us to impose our will and our values on others. If they resisted, we had the war machines to quell their resistance. Americans were the leaders of the free world. I think you Sioux children recognise the America that I am talking about?

But everything goes in cycles; empires perish; civilisations rise and then inevitably fall, to be replaced by new civilisations. Gradually it came about that the rest of the world was no longer willing to follow the lead of the United States without question. A day came when the emerging new masters of the universe decided that the power of America needed to be restricted and that Americans should be put in their place, just as those Americans had once decreed that we Indians should be restricted to the places allocated to us – the reservations. On these USA reservations, people had been provided with whatever would keep them passive and compliant. So there were MacDonalds, Dunkin' Do-nuts, the baseball stadiums, and other such necessities of the American way of life, so that there would be limited resistance to the new regime which was being imposed by the world rulers."

The old story teller sighed and blinked at them through her milky cataracts.

"Think about this, children. Do not let yourselves be overawed by the might of America, which is transient. Have faith in your own heritage and values and strive to find ways to keep our culture alive in this ever-changing world."

THE DILEMMA

Moira Newlan

Staff were expected to work irregular hours, involving early mornings or late into the night. Exposure to frost, biting rain, high winds and winter gloom were part of it all, for which, it had to be said they were handsomely paid.

The shifts suited Susie — she had never liked predictable routines. Now that she was a mother, the benefits had become even more pronounced. Her husband could share their son Archie's care without relying on favours from the wider family. Susie would have preferred to have taken the maximum maternity leave, but had bowed to pressure to return after only three months to cope with the new demands at Border Control. She had been one of just a handful of employees selected to train in supervising the Government's new Brexit plan. It had been a compliment and brought prestige, but not something she would have chosen at that time. The training had involved understanding the new rules and regulations and software programmes, changes in the legal procedures and all the paper work involved. The layers of bureaucracy were astonishing, but she was obliged to just to follow the rules, not to question them. The port's physical appearance had been transformed beyond recognition in the last eighteen months; new lanes, new multi-lingual signs, new kiosks erected at strategic points over the concourse.

One part of her work which had not changed though, was the thorough checking of all types of vehicles for stowaways. Since the Syrian civil war, this had become part of the daily routine. It was surprising how versatile, inventive and daringly imaginative individuals could be. Desperation drove them, she knew. In the early days, a colleague had found six people huddled together in a refrigerated unit. It was just by chance that the driver had noticed an irregularity with the temperature gauge and had gone to check his vehicle. Back then, none of us would have even considered it necessary to check a refrigerated cargo. But now . . .

Although the checks were as comprehensive as possible, Susie knew that there was an element of chance. With staff shortages, extreme pressure of numbers and human error someone could be missed. This led to hope, she assumed, for those attempting the crossing. She herself was painstakingly thorough; undercarriages, cabins, boots, crates, seats, cargo.

One day, not long after she had returned to work, Susie was checking a Spanish container, with its cargo of oils, preserved meats and oranges, bound, she supposed for a supermarket warehouse. She was about to signal to the driver to prepare to depart, when she realised that several of the oranges had been displaced, wedged so tightly between the crates that they had begun to seep. Then she noticed an almost imperceptible gap in one of those boxed containers. Instinct told her to shine her torch into the small pool of darkness created when the fruit had been dislodged. A glint of an iris, the white of teeth, a moment of silence. As she carefully removed the surrounding oranges, a small, hunched figure was revealed. It was difficult to guess the age or the ethnicity, but easy to feel the terror. Susie felt a wave of sympathy, compassion, and protectiveness wash over her. These were new feelings, motherhood had changed her. Instead of shouting for assistance, Susie was now considering what to do. Should she simply cover up the crate and give the all-clear, letting this desperate individual take their chances, away from government control to a freedom of sorts? Or should she turn them in to the authorities. A grim stay in a detention camp would follow. It might take months for their case to be heard. Even then they might be sent back. But at least there would be regular meals, a clean bed and health and dental checks. Which choice, she wondered, would best help this poor creature?

Gently, she created a larger space around the figure, chatting as if to her own child. She remembered the uneaten chocolate bar in her pocket and pressed it into the curled hands.

That evening, Susie acknowledged that maternity had altered her being in some profound way. Her doubt and ambivalence had taken her by surprise and she now questioned her career choice. She had to believe that the young man she had found would find a place somehow, be integrated into this new society and be able to live a better life. But she could never be sure.

THE TOWN HOUSE
Nicola L C Talbot

George Arbuthnot gazed through the sash window at the people walking along the street outside. What strange clothes they wore, both in the style and the unnaturalness of the materials. Long boots with a smooth sheen. Was that supposed to be some kind of tunic without breeches? With their brightly coloured garments, metal bracelets, amber beaded necklaces, and long hair, they looked vaguely Celtish.

Opposite was a tall, grey building—not the elegance of a grey Portland stone edifice built along classical styles, but an ugly tower with small windows that cast a shadow across the street.

When George had first moved into his town house—when had that been? Eighty-four? No, eighty-three—there had been a terrace opposite that mirrored George's side, but it had been demolished in that frightful explosion—so loud that it had woken George from a deep slumber up in the attic where he had retreated after the unpleasant encounter with that awful medium pest.

Oh, didn't I mention? George was — how can one put this delicately — *corporeally challenged.*

He had moved here in 1783, along with Gladys the parlourmaid and Hargreave, who had kept all nuisance visitors away and had managed things in such a way that George was able to concentrate on his books and essays without being bothered by mundane matters. There had been other servants in the household, but Hargreave had dealt with all that kind of thing.

13

For a while, everything had seemed just right, and—more often than not—George spent his time reading and writing in the parlour, until his household arrangements were disrupted by the loss of Gladys, some damn fool had knocked her down whilst racing along the street in his gig.

It was the only time that George had been prompted to write a letter to his Member of Parliament to demand that something be done to curtail such reckless behaviour. George even went so far as to venture outside and paid a visit to the honourable gentleman when he failed to produce a satisfactory response. What's more, during that unsavoury interval, George had even spoken to his solicitor about the matter, rather than delegating the whole affair to Hargreave.

'Really, I don't know why you've got yourself so worked up about it all,' his solicitor replied. 'I know it happened right on your doorstep, but these events are always occurring, and no one has identified the fellow in question, so it will be virtually impossible to pursue reparation.'

'Reparation? Don't you understand? I've lost my parlourmaid.'

'But, Mr Arbuthnot, there are plenty of maids. Just get another one and forget about the whole business.'

So a new parlourmaid arrived, and after a few years there was another, and then in time yet another, but none of them were quite adequate. Not that George was able to explain to Hargreave exactly what was wrong with them, other than the fact that they weren't Gladys. Even George had to concede that was hardly their fault.

The parlour no longer seemed as comfortable as it had once been, and George found he was able to work better in his study. His particular interest was antiquities—Roman, Celtic, Pict—so long as it had been buried for several hundred years and then dug up again—by someone other than George.

He hardly noticed the years go by, until he found it hard to read small inscriptions, his knees grew stiff, and his back began to ache.

Hargreave had less hair and, when George looked in a mirror, he realised he had less too.

Then one day Hargreave fell over. He was carried to his room, but one side of his face had fallen, like a waxwork figure left too close to the fire. A physician came, but shook his head and said that nothing could be done.

What was George to do without Hargreave? He was beset by people asking him questions and telling him things, until one day a stabbing pain in his chest forced him to sit down and his body never stood up again.

The afterlife guide turned up and told George about a place he could go to. When George heard that Gladys and Hargreave were already there, his initial reluctance to leave his home was overcome. Of course, if his old servants were also there . . .

'No, you misunderstand,' the afterlife guide interrupted. 'There are no servants over there. All are friends.'

'But who will make the tea and light the fire?' was all that George could manage to say.

'If you want a blazing fire, an alternative place is available.'

George didn't much care for the afterlife guide's tone of voice. No, he wasn't leaving. This was his home, with all his books and antiquities. So here he stayed.

For the first few days, everything seemed just right. No one pestered him, but he found he couldn't pick up his books too well and kept dropping them on the floor. So, he decided to simply sit in a chair for a while, but servants came and threw covers over the furniture and bolted fast the shutters, leaving George in the dark. Then men arrived and packed things up in boxes and removed all the furniture.

'Not my books! My antiquities!'

They stripped the house bare. George drifted from one room to another. He was entirely alone.

After some time, new furniture was brought in, the shutters were unbolted, and the first of the pests infested his home. A young couple arrived and there was so much commotion and so many visitors that George took himself off to a dark corner of the attic. Much to his delight, he discovered a forgotten case of antiquities and, for a while, occupied himself with cataloguing them, but he had no way of writing down his findings. So he imagined that he was sitting in the parlour with a cup of tea that Gladys had just brought, and he described his discoveries to her, as he had so often done before. She'd had a keen eye for detail, asked intelligent questions, and could always remember the names of runes and to which period they belonged.

Eventually he returned downstairs to see what the pests had done to the place. The furniture was elegant enough, but this chair should be over here not there, and these ornaments will be knocked over if left on those little tables. They ought to be put in that cabinet over there to keep them safe.

The pests turned out to be quite ungrateful about his assistance and moved everything back again. Spring came round, and the pests went off in a carriage. The furniture was covered and the shutters were bolted again.

At least George had some peace and quiet now and felt able to explore his home more freely. There was a grand pianoforte in the parlour. George lifted up the dust cover and ran his fingers over the woodwork.

He'd had an upright piano in this corner of the room—not that he'd ever played it. He had inherited it from a great-aunt. Gladys had dusted it most prodigiously, even to the point of dusting the individual keys—not from one end to the other, but here and there, making a pleasant tune. She had been embarrassed on discovering that he had observed, but, as George told her, if she wished to play it there was surely no harm in that. When she confessed to not knowing how, George had instructed Hargreave to find someone to teach her.

Hargreave had raised an eyebrow, as he had a habit of doing, but he had replied that he would endeavour to find a way, as though George had tasked him with fetching a golden fleece.

After Gladys was lost, the instrument had remained untouched, and now it was gone—probably to one of his nieces. He raised the lid of this new, larger and grander instrument and brushed his fingers over the keys, trying to remember how Gladys had played that first time he had heard her. If her untutored fingers had found the right notes, why couldn't his? If only he had asked for lessons for himself as well. Surely it was this key here and then that one.

He stopped as he heard footsteps. The housekeeper came in and stared in George's direction. She picked up a poker and jabbed it under the dust sheets. George fled back to the attic.

The couple returned in the autumn, but the husband seemed rarely indoors. They had certainly disarranged George's home with their furniture and accessories, but it was still a comfortable abode, so why should anyone want to be constantly going out and coming back so late? If he didn't care for the place then he should quit it and leave George in peace.

One evening, thinking the house empty, George entered the parlour to find the lady sitting there alone, her head bent over a book in her lap, but on closer inspection he realised she wasn't reading it, but was touching some dried petals that had been concealed between two pages.

She seemed so forlorn that George, not knowing what else to do, placed his hand on her shoulder, in what he considered an avuncular manner. She slapped the book shut with a cry of terror and George raced back to the attic.

The man, when he was home, became increasingly irksome, raising his voice and thumping about. George tried to ignore the noise as he hid in the attic with his last remaining box of antiquities, but it was no use. He dashed downstairs, determined to find some way to make his displeasure known, and found the couple in the parlour just in time to witness the man strike his wife.

'You ruffian,' George said and, though he had never had any practice in such matters, swung a punch straight at the man.

His fist passed through the man's head, yet it must have had some impact as the fellow staggered back in shock.

'You, sir, are an unmitigated scoundrel,' George continued, lunging for the poker, but somehow he couldn't quite gain a firm hold of it. The poker clattered against the other fire irons and fell on the hearth. The lady screamed and fled from the room.

It wasn't long after that that the entire household moved out, along with all the furniture, and George was left in peace—but not for long.

The next pest to infest his home was an elderly dowager. The moment George saw her, he was filled with a terror that he would be stuck with a cantankerous housemate who might refuse to move on when her time came. It became a matter of priority that he evict this pest as soon as possible. He moved things around and knocked things over, but she would simply scold him, as though he were a mischievous child, and kept addressing him as 'Henry'.

Eventually George felt that he had no choice but to resort to more extreme measures. He placed his hand on her shoulder, much as he had done to the previous lady, but this time she sighed and said: 'Oh, Henry!' A tear rolled down her cheek, the sight of it so mortified George that he retreated back to the attic.

One morning the dowager failed to get out of bed. George fidgeted as a young woman sat by the old lady's side, holding her hand. It was too late now. There'd be no getting rid of her, but when the afterlife guide turned up for her, neither paid the slightest attention to George. She floated away, looking more like a bride than a dowager, intent on being reunited with her Henry.

Other pests came and went, some more irksome than others, but the worst was the medium who arrived wearing a cloche hat and fur-trimmed coat. Purple silks and long velvet drapes were soon hung up around the parlour, which was bad enough, but the sheer indignity of being ordered about to join in her silly games was beyond the pale. It wasn't George who jiggled her lace-covered table in front of her visitors, that's for sure.

He returned to the attic and settled down for a long sleep until he was awoken by the explosion that demolished the house opposite. At first it was too dark to tell what was going on. The medium and her purple hangings were gone. Now all the windows had black blinds pulled down. He discovered that a new set of pests were infesting his cellar, but his irritation over the invasion of his home was softened by their terrified expressions.

Morning came, and George discovered that the stained glass from his fanlight lay in scattered fragments on the floor, and the front door hung lopsidedly on its hinges, but that was nothing to the sight across the road: mounds of rubble and a fireplace halfway up a lonely wall with the remnant of a hearth beneath it. People were searching through the debris and carrying covered mounds away on stretchers.

George's front door was repaired, but the fanlight was simply boarded up. As far as he could tell, some fellow called Jerry was attacking, with some excessively large cannon-balls, at night. George decided not to try his usual tricks with the new occupants, reasoning that the explosions and caterwauling sirens were far more terrifying than anything he could do. Instead, he sat with them whenever they had to retreat to the cellar in order to keep them company in the event that the afterlife guide, who must be fearfully busy, was delayed. He had it all planned out, how he would introduce himself and reassure them, and he prepared talks of varying lengths, depending on how long a wait they might have to endure.

The household consisted of an elderly couple, a younger woman who George soon guessed was their daughter, and a young girl who seemed to be the sum total of their domestic staff. George learnt that the daughter had a husband, who was fighting 'the nasties' (although perhaps he misunderstood this because their accent was a little strange) and they had three children who were away in the country. He rejoiced with the family every time a letter arrived to reassure them that loved ones were still alive and well, and offered words of condolence whenever a black-bordered letter arrived. But most of all, he was utterly overjoyed when the husband and children returned home, even though it meant the house was full of noise and chatter.

The children grew up and the family moved out. The house looked so shabby now with blistered paintwork and rotting frames. The smashed fanlight had been replaced with a dull clouded pane. The early morning sun no longer splashed colour across the wall but instead seeped dimly through the glass. Once the grey tower block was built, no more sunlight reached the fanlight any more.

Men came in with tools, and began hammering and smashing and sawing, but they weren't restoring the house, they were adding new walls, splitting up rooms and blocking up fireplaces. Worst of all, they found George's last box of antiquities.

'Give them back, you thieves. They're mine.'

But George couldn't make them hear him and was unable to snatch the box back. He fumed and ranted and raged. Eventually the men left, leaving behind them drab, mean rooms. The parlour was ruined, so George remained in the attic. He paced the rafters while new pests arrived to infest his home. This time he was going to evict them all. Make them restore his house. Teach them a lesson for ruining his home.

Finally, he felt himself ready to do battle. He descended from the attic and went into the room that had once been his study, where he found a baby in a cot and a woman sleeping on a hard bed nearby. The room was cluttered with clothes-horses, from which wet laundry hung: nappies, sheets and baby garments. George quietly retreated and went downstairs to the remains of his parlour. Where the fireplace had once been was now a metal contraption with two bars, one of which glowed orange. An old woman sat huddled in front of it, wrapped in a blanket. The room smelt damp and stale. George gazed out of the sash window at the long-haired woman in a nylon mini-dress and vinyl boots walking by in the shadow of the grey tower block.

Was there any way of finding the place the afterlife guide had spoken of? If only he could find Gladys and Hargreave. George would be quite content to make the tea and light the fire if only he could be with them again. He headed for the door, and, for the first time in over a hundred years, George left the house.

COLOURS IN TROOPING THE COLOUR

Patrick Linehan

"Black!" shouted the Regimental Sergeant Major.

"Sah!" answered Black, and was off his bed and erect to attention in one swift, practised movement.

"Colour!" screamed the RSM. "You're carrying it, though Gawd knows why. You're thin; you're scrawny; I 'ad a whole bleedin' regiment to pick from but they didn't ask me an' if they 'ad —!" He shook his head in sorrow, "Your saving grace – and no credit to you — is that you're lanky enough; so get your kit on; report to me."

With that, he executed a staccato three point turn in high sheen black boots, and barrelled through the door.

When Black got to the office, he was asked, "Can you read?"

"Yes, Sah!" he said, and was handed a sheet of one-line instructions.

"Read it. Live it. Sleep it. Then eat it — for you won't have it for comfort on the day. Clear?"

"Sah!" he said.

The colour — the banner — was not just one colour. The background was red; superimposed across that, the regimental emblems stood out in gold relief, all within a gold border. It had a Union Jack – red white and blue – in a corner. And it had a pole of light brown wood.

And so the rehearsals began. A first lonely march was a cock-up; well they would say that. The RSM's face, with its small, red-rimmed eyes; its blonde-to-gingery eye lashes; its purple nose was yelling in his. And he had halitosis! That, he thought, could only be slimy green.

Black kept his own eyes open. To close them, hide their blue, and it would be seen as weakness. He reflected that whenever he had been this close to anyone his eyes would have been shut, mostly in ecstasy, and he latched on to the sometime softness of that.

The rehearsals became the daily grind, the subject of sympathy or green-eyed ridicule by his mates; and he could tell which would have the colourless venom to be the RSMs of the future. At last, he was ready for the march in the Mall.

First dress rehearsal under his belt and the crimson chasm of the RSM's mouth issuing a bawling, "You're not an 'orse; lift your feet!" Just because he'd kicked a yellow gravel pebble; but he thought the tone, somehow, softer. Then the second 'dress' flawless, he knew. The RSM knew otherwise but wouldn't — couldn't — say why.

Finally, the big day. His mother and sister, in an overnight hotel, their blue hats and cottage-garden dresses hanging in clinging, clear, plastic sheaths. They slept little. In the early morning they saw, as he did, the roseate dawn suffuse a grey and glassy London City.

For him, red dress uniform, again; people helping him to brass his buttons; to smooth the hints of peplum and pleat in the jacket; to check the bear-black busby.

Hours later, as he stood rigidly to attention on the Mall, the Queen, her light-blue complementing the darker hue of her carriage, passed him, and he could have sworn she winked at him. "There," he thought. "Slide that to the purple roots of your RSM's varicose veins."

OUTSIDE THE BOX

Shirley Buxton

This room is a box, a bright, white, clinical box. It's my new home. My children left saying they would be back, bringing pictures, photos, books and other treasures to make it feel more homely, but I am beginning to think that is not what I want. Perhaps I want a holiday from reality. Perhaps I don't want to be reminded of the last few months.

Let me give you a guided tour of 'My Box'. To the left is a wall with a window and to my right a wall with two doors. In front of me is just a blank wall. I am anchored on a bed, floating on an ocean. Rafted beside me are a compact chest-of-drawers and an armchair. I can't see behind me but it must be another blank wall, but I don't want to dwell on that. What I can't see seems rather daunting, perhaps even scary. At the moment, it is my wall of worry and uncertainty. Best to focus on what I can see, what is in front of me.

Imagining that I can, I extend my arm towards the facing wall and press lightly with my forefinger. Instantly that side of my box flips silently down releasing a welcome wave of warm, humid air into my sterile surroundings. My ears are assaulted with a cacophony of sound. Unthinking, I swing my legs to the ground and stroll into the rain-forest that stretches out before me. The power of nature envelops me. The complexity of this unique eco-system is overwhelming. It is a world teaming with life. The dense canopy above filters the burning sun. The vivid colours of exuberant blooms are caught up by vocal parrots, and carried through the air on butterfly wings. There is nothing here to threaten me. Every creature is intent in their own business. I am a world apart. My body is re-vitalised. I am made whole. The body, damaged by age, is healed and my balance restored. I can dodge the tangled tree roots, climb mossy boulders and wade through cooling streams. There is a lull in the forest sound and from the distance I hear my name. I follow the call and at once I am back on my bed with the wall closing upon my thinking.

Over the following days that wall drops down many times, allowing the world to flood into my room and draw me out of my confinement. I see the sun rise over the River Nile, the great river's gentle currents carrying me from the ancient tombs of the Pharaohs to the Temple of Philae. I see the sun set over the rugged snow-capped Dolomites. In the Land of the Midnight Sun, I experience the stunning spectacle of the Aurora Borealis. I swim with fish through coral forests and clamber over desert dunes.

Today that wall is firmly closed. I look at the wall to my left, the one with a window framing a handsome tree. I reach out; a light touch and wall falls away. The cherry tree, clad in autumn flames, stands in a well-tended garden with a path leading down to a road. A car waits by the gate, my faithful blue Ford Focus. I climb in, start the engine and drive into my past. Familiar faces and places comfort me. I feel at ease. I am suddenly aware that my young children are sitting on the back seat squabbling over peppermints. They are filled with excitement and enthusiasm, eager to explore new places as we Youth Hostel together in the Derbyshire Peaks. Sun glints on golden leaves, freshly filled steams tumble and spill over rocky ledges and the river valley calls us to meander along its paths and climb its grassy banks together.

All too soon, the calling of my name transports me back to 'My Box.' Wistfully, I hope on another day the old beige Prefect with its indicator arms will be parked behind that left wall, waiting to journey me back to my own childhood.

You may wonder about the wall with two doors on my right. I suppose it is the 'right' wall. It is the wall of present, of reality. It reveals the world of the wonderful people who care for us. One door leads to an *en-suite*. I've been too weak to venture in there. The other door leads out towards the kitchens where staff prepare our meals. There is the sluice room with bedpans and commodes. Tall linen cupboards line one side of the corridor while on this side there are doors, lots of doors leading to bright white clinical boxes, just like mine. I long to open those doors and speak with the people inside. I want to tell them about the mystical qualities of the walls in this place. I want to know the freedom they can have but I am not allowed. It is forbidden. Perhaps they will discover these wonders for themselves.

I've escaped again, this time a plane has whisked me to the palm-fringed beaches of Mauritius, where I walk upon silver sands with crystal-clear waters lapping over my toes. It was under this sun that I was married. What happiness I found here so many years ago. I glance over my shoulder to see if my husband is there.

'Grandma.'

I am pulled back into the present. My granddaughter is by my side, holding my hand. She has brought my great grandchildren. Baby Clara rests peacefully in her other arm. I catch sight of two-year-old Tommy disappearing under the foot of my bed. There is much giggling, a second or two of hush and then from behind me:

'BOO! Hello Great-Nan. It's ME!'

Tears of relief fill my eyes. That back wall is solid. It is the 'Wall of Love'. All my fears have gone. Tommy has revealed what is behind me. It is my family and my friends. I look up, beyond the ceiling above, and give grateful, heartfelt thanks.

VANCE

Stuart McCarthy

The town sweltered beneath the hot desert sun. All was quiet. The main street was flanked on either side by weatherboard buildings each fronted by a covered veranda. There was the livery stable, that took up much of the far end of the street, and the general store, hotel, saloon, bath house and sheriff's office competed for space in the rest.

The silence was broken by the shuffling clop of a lone horse and rider. The man, tall in the saddle, hat pulled down and bandana pulled up to protect his face from the sun and dust, stopped outside the saloon. He dismounted and tied his horse to the rail and ascended the steps. He was stopped by an outstretched leg.

'Howdy,' said the owner of the leg. He was sitting just outside the swing doors of the saloon and had been watching the stranger as he rode through. The star pinned to his shirt gave weight and the six-gun in his right hand sent the clear message 'Don't mess with me.'

'Care to state your business, boy,' he continued.

'Beer, bath, bed then move on in the morning.'

'You got a name, boy?'

'Vance.'

'OK Vance, livery stable at the far end, ten cents a night, hotel next to it and bath house next to that. Saloon is right here.'

The sheriff moved his leg to let Vance pass.

Vance looked up and down the street, fixing each landmark in his mind. Looked at the sheriff.

'Thanks,' he said.

'You take care in there,' said the sheriff.

'Thanks,' said Vance again.

Vance passed inside. The saloon was quiet, only the bartender behind the bar and three others sitting at a table in a corner. They were playing cards, all wore guns. They exchanged glances and nodded to Vance as he stepped up to the bar. Vance returned the nods.

'What can I get you?' asked the bartender.

'Beer and a quiet place to drink it.'

The bartender poured the drink and pointed to a table in the opposite corner from the card players.

'Thanks,' said Vance and went to the table.

Seated, the hardships of the trail seemed to dissolve away. He sipped his beer. Yes, he thought, a beer and then a long soak and a soft bed and he would be part of the human race again. Then he would be ready to move on to whatever would come next.

'Say fellers,' came a harsh voice from the opposite side of the room, 'can you smell something in here?'

'Yeh,' the other two answered, 'wonder where it's coming from.'

'I reckon it's coming from over there,' he said, pointing. 'Hey, you, pig-sty, you fouling up our air?'

Vance lifted his hat brim with a finger, looked across the room, and then lowered the brim and returned to his drink.

'Hey, pig-sty, I'm talking to you. We don't like our air being fouled. What you going to do about it?'

No answer.

The three card players rose as one man and strode towards Vance.

The bartender discovered he had things to do in the store room and left hurriedly.

One of the card players stood by the door and watched the sheriff, making sure he couldn't intervene in what was about to happen. Such things didn't happen often, and entertainment was where you found it.

The leader was now standing in front of Vance. He sniffed the air loudly.

'Yeh, pig-sty, it is you. You stink. This saloon is only for clean people.' He bent closer to take a good sniff but his head jerked back; he had come face to face with the barrel of a loaded six gun.

'You got a problem with me mister?' said Vance in a quiet, dangerously quiet voice.

The man stepped back, hand reaching for his gun.

'I wouldn't,' said Vance.

'You're pretty fast with that aintcha,' said the leader, his voice quavering. He had never had a reaction like that before and it worried him.

'Faster than you.'

'Care to prove it?' His words didn't match his inner feelings.

'Nope.' Vance holstered his gun and stood to leave.

'You ain't goin' nowhere,' blustered the leader, 'we got a score to settle.'

'No, we don't,' replied Vance evenly, picked up his saddle bags and made for the door.

The leader pulled his gun and fanned back the hammer as he had been practising and squeezed the trigger. He was about to say 'Yes we do,' when his gun hand exploded into a spray of blood and smashed bone. Vance, gun in hand, looked at the others. 'Anyone else wanna try?'

The silence from the others gave him the answer.

'Get him to a doctor.' Vance pointed to the injured man who was kneeling, crying with pain; his gun slinging days over before they had even begun.

Outside the sheriff spoke to him.

'Leaving so soon?'

'Place doesn't suit me. Guess I'll be moving on. You heard?'

'I heard.'

'Anything else?'

'Don't think so.'

'So long sheriff.'

'So long Vance, you take care now.'

The silence of the desert returned as the shuffling clop of the horse retreated into the distance.

THE MAGIC BEACH

Alison Court

The day was golden. The sky was blue, the sea a millpond, wavelets lapping onto the beach with just the faintest of murmurs. The scent of the pines from the dunes behind them touched the air. The Family Stern was setting off to make this the most splendid of all beach days, their very last in this secluded spot. For Great Uncle Martin was selling up, house, beach and all.

But not every member of the family seemed to be enjoying it. Oma fussed with her chair.

"It won't stay upright. There's too much wind. And the sun is blinding." She held her sketch pad in her hand and her watercolours, but oh dear, where were her brushes?

Erica tried to pacify her, "Mother, I'll go back to the house and find them. Just sit with your book a little while."

"But I wanted to knit, knitting is so much easier than painting, on the beach. Oh dear, oh dear, where, oh where, can my knitting be now, do you suppose? Some gnarled old fisherman will have found it and thrown it back overboard, I'm sure."

Meanwhile Opa, dressed as always in the summer months in his venerable panama hat and his ivory linen summer jacket, struggled with his easel. Would any other eighty-year-old attempt to paint in oils on a sandy beach? Surely not. It was all the fault of those blasted Impressionists, heroes of his youth, and their *en plein air*.

"Confounded thing," he muttered, as yet again the easel lurched and his canvas fell into the sand. "Thundering blistering barnacles."

But Ilse and her friend Amandine were blissfully happy. They had already swum out to the rocks where they spent every day discovering rock pools or searching for crabs. They filled their buckets time and time again, to peer and wonder at the life and form of a myriad of sea creatures, before tipping them back into their watery homes.

The boys, Caspar and David, ran up and down the shore with their shrimping nets. "Come on, if we work hard, we'll have enough for everyone for lunch."

When they had done with shrimping, they planned to dig the biggest hole in the world. And they hadn't even been in the water yet. There was so much to do on their magic beach, and the day stretched out in front of them and their horizons reached far.

Friedrich, their father, had already taken himself off to an outcrop, where he perched with his fishing rod. He was a silent father, loving his family very tenderly, but happiest when in contemplative mood and silently gazing at his line. Mackerel were his daily catch and the family's omega levels were high, after a week of fishy suppers.

Erica, their mother, busied herself with the mountains of food she had brought to feed the family on a long day at the beach. The windbreak shielded a delicious lunch, laid out on a quilt; loaves of bread, half a dozen different cheeses, fillets of herring in sour cream, hard-boiled eggs, kilos of tomatoes, giant jars of gherkins, piles of apples and cherries, and the strudel and streusel she had baked that morning, before everyone got up.

And there was Great Uncle Martin clambering down the steep wooden steps on the dunes, megaphone in hand.

"What on earth has he got a megaphone for? Whatever will he do next?" worried Erica. She was always just a hint nervous when

Martin was around, unpredictability being his guiding principle. He ambled up to the group assembled on the beach, and threw himself down onto the quilt, narrowly avoiding the cheese, probably only by chance. He reached for a loaf and started to tear the end from it.

"Martin, NO, wait for everyone else, please," scolded Erica. But she couldn't be cross for long on a day like this, and she turned a blind eye when he took no notice of her. At least he hadn't tucked into the cheese, or the cake.

Oma was settled now. She looked like she was nodding off, under her straw hat, her book fallen to the sand at her feet. It had been most unfortunate, yesterday, her knitting floating out to sea like that. Erica smiled to herself. It had been funny, really, but better that no one knew she thought that! And Opa, well, he was still muttering to himself, but now it was about his painting, which looked like it might be one of his better ones. Erica hoped it would be; he had promised she should have it when it was done, a view of the islands lying out in the Baltic, a memento of this last ever holiday on their beloved beach.

For now, she sat back peacefully, a quiet moment to enjoy the shimmering blue air. The children were happily engaged in their various pursuits; she was free to muse on her own thoughts of the bedtime book she was enjoying so much, the great classic Effi Briest, set on this very stretch of coast. Martin didn't need any response to his chuntering, he was perfectly happy to carry on regardless of whether anyone was listening. (Usually they weren't, because he mostly talked about swords, or battleships, which no one else in the family was very interested in or knowledgeable about.)

"ACH!!!" He'd picked up his megaphone. "GET OFF THOSE DUNES!" he bellowed, and there, clambering amongst the dunes, below the pine trees, was a young couple laughing and slithering in the sand. "GET OFF THOSE DUNES!" The young couple stopped, looking bewildered at the sudden interruption.

"YOU DEGRADE THIS HALLOWED ENVIRONMENT," Martin bellowed again, and the young couple turned and fled.

That was their day spoiled, thought Erica sadly, but she hurriedly diverted further unpleasantness by calling out, "Lunch is ready," and incredibly, something happened that never happened when they were at home: every single member of the family dropped what they were doing and gathered hungrily beside the quilt.

They tucked in, ravenously. There's nothing like fresh seaside air for stirring an appetite. At last, they had eaten their fill and were lying back, satisfied, when, out of the blue, Great Uncle Martin roared, "I'VE GOT A LITTLE SURPRISE FOR YOU YOUNG 'UNS LATER." Erica raised an eyebrow and felt a shiver of anxiety; what would that be? She looked over to Friedrich for reassurance, but he was taking no notice of the implicit threat in Martin's declaration. Instead, he was setting off with the boys to dig their famous hole. The moment subsided. The girls went back to their rockpools, the grandparents settled for a nap, Erica closed her eyes.

The afternoon passed. It was a perfect last day. The hole was the biggest ever. The haul of mackerel grew. Ilse and Amandine led the party up to the pine woods to collect kindling for the evening's bonfire. They gathered a good pile, and, as the sun started to go down, Great Uncle Martin set it alight, still chuckling over his promised "treat". The boys joined in and stoked the fire. The girls wrapped potatoes in foil and pushed them into the heart of the heat, there to bake ready for supper. Supper would indeed be delicious, with the mackerel, supplementing the slightly meagre haul of shrimps, now filleted and in a frying pan, sizzling on top of the fire.

As the sun went below the horizon, over to the west, all was quiet. It had been a beautiful last day and everyone was contented.

Suddenly, Oma sat bolt upright, "Beware — jellyfish!" Ilse ran to where she was pointing and bent down to pick up, not a jellyfish, but her grandmother's knitting, dripping wet and soaked in sand. Amidst the happy sound of rejoicing, there was a tremendous crack in the air, a single bolt of thunder, and there was Martin, his arm up in the air, with a REVOLVER.

"There, I told you I'd got a bit of a surprise for you," he exulted, "my gun from the war. I thought that would liven up your day a little!"

Hubbub and horror. To everyone's amazement, Friedrich leapt at Martin and grabbed the gun - with some ease, luckily, for Martin was, after all, an old man.

"Steady on, steady on," countered Martin, but even he knew he might have gone too far this time.

"Time to pack up, then," said Erica, "We're going home."

They gathered up the remains of the day. Laden with bags and chairs, quilts and windbreaks, buckets and spades and fishing tackle, they silently trooped back up the beach in the darkness, up the rickety wooden steps, and over the dunes. There they turned one last time and gazed back over their beloved magic beach, scene of so many happy summer days. The imprint of the perfect scene engraved on each of their memories, again they turned, and took the path through the woods, to wind their way back home.

It had been a day that they knew they would never forget.

CAMPING ON BEAR MOUNTAIN
Avril Suddaby

It was a dark and stormy night . . . I hope you'll forgive the corny beginning but Bertie won't have it any other way. Whenever I try to tell him a story with a different beginning he gets upset. So let it stand.

It was indeed a dark and windy night when we (that is, Bertie and me, Jake) went camping on a snowy New Year's Eve on what Bertie had, for some reason, decided to call 'Bear Mountain'. I go along with him on this because it seems important to him even though there are, of course, no wild bears in this country. Bertie and I live next door to each other in sheltered housing and I am, by default, Bertie's carer. He was discharged from the army 12 years ago with PTSD. He suffers from claustrophobia, as a result of being injured while on active service, and he has short-term memory problems. Since I came back from Africa I've suffered badly from depression, and it helps me to look after Bertie. Not that he's really any trouble, but he can't go out alone and has panic attacks if he's in a situation where there's what he calls a crowd (meaning more than half a dozen people). He can't even cope with going to church with me; I've tried but it was too much for him, despite the pitifully small numbers in church nowadays. However, we're both physically very fit, probably because we go to our allotment most days. Bertie needs to be out in the open air and it does me good too.

Now that the introductions are done, I should explain how we came to be spending New Year's Eve camping in the snow. Well, last summer we went hiking in the National Park. It was a hot day and we were running low on water, so when we came to a camp, I left Bertie in a quiet spot where no one would bother him and went to buy a bottle of water from the camp shop. When I came back he was unusually talkative.

"When I was in the army," he said, "I sometimes went camping."

"Tell me about it, Bertie," I said. "Was it sort of like a holiday, when you had leave?"

"No, no, not a holiday," he said vehemently. "We were doing training. Not like these people camping. That's not real camping. Look at them with their enormous tents, their tables and chairs and parasols and BBQ's. When we went camping we had to carry everything on our backs."

"Where did you go camping, Bertie?" I asked. "Can you remember?"

"I can't remember the names. Not places like this with showers and toilets and shops. We camped in faraway places where there were no other people. It was great."

"Did you sometimes camp when the weather was bad, Bertie?"

"Yeh, even in the snow. I liked it best of all when it was cold. Hot weather makes you all sweaty and uncomfortable when you're carrying a heavy rucksack."

So somehow, from this discussion we ended up planning to do some 'real camping' next winter. If I had thought Bertie would just forget about it, the way he forgets so many things now, I was mistaken. He just kept on and on about it, so I thought why not give it a go. Why the winter, rather than the summer, you're probably wondering. Well, in the winter there's not much to do at the allotment so we are often at a loose end, with time on our hands. Also in the summer, camping in the National Park is only possible in crowded camp sites, like the one I just told you about. That would give Bertie the heebie-jeebies. And if you try to do wild camping anywhere in the Park, the Rangers pretty soon find you and move you on. It's a very regulated country we live in with too much red tape and too many rules. So we finally decided to camp on New Year's Eve when any nosy Park Ranger would be at home celebrating.

It took us a long time to get all the stuff together. It brought back all sorts of memories for Bertie as he inspected everything, rejecting many of the items I'd borrowed or bought, as too heavy and cumbersome, or just plain unnecessary. I wanted good equipment because it would probably be cold. I knew the cold wouldn't bother Bertie as he's tough as old boots, he always sleeps next to an open window, summer and winter, and never seems to feel the cold. The only camping I'd ever done was in Africa, and certainly, at least as far as temperature was concerned, it was a bit different from our northern hemisphere in winter.

After Christmas was over, we prepared our rucksacks. Bertie was to carry the small two-man tent with aluminium poles, the primus and the shovel. He insisted on that bloody shovel, I wasn't sure why. I had to carry the sleeping mats and sleeping bags and our provisions for an evening meal and New Year's Day breakfast. Although my rucksack looked bulkier and heavier than Bertie's it actually weighed less. On December 31st my mate, Dave, gave us a lift to the National Park in his car and then wished us well and left us with a promise to come and pick us up at the same spot on New Year's Day.

We strapped on the snow shoes and set off. It's hard walking in snow shoes but with a heavy load on your back it's even more demanding. I was soon sweating and to think that I had worried before about being cold. We went steadily upwards, up the southern slope of Bear Mountain. We stopped once to eat our sandwiches when the sun came out and the world was white, clean and beautiful in the sparkling snow. We walked for several hours and saw only deer, a fox in his off-white winter coat and an eagle circling overhead. I've never before seen Bertie so at ease and at one with his surroundings. Normally I'm the one who sets the pace and takes decisions but here our roles were reversed.

At last Bertie stopped, "I think this would be a good place to camp. The cliff there will give us some shelter and we should get the tent up before bad weather comes."

He was right. Looking over towards the cliff I could see dark clouds gathering and a wind was getting up. We put down our rucksacks and Bertie got to work with the shovel, telling me that we had to make a hollow (seemed more like a pit to me) for the tent, which might otherwise be blown away by the wind.

If walking had been hard, shovelling snow was even harder. Whenever Bertie got tired and needed a rest I took over for a few minutes. At last he was satisfied with the our work, the pit was about the size of a kid's paddling pool. "That's fine," he said. "Now you see if you can find some dryish wood to make a fire while I put up the tent."

My fire wasn't a success. All the wood I could find was damp and the wind was getting stronger and soon blew out any semblance of a flame. My dreams of sitting by a campfire drinking whisky and swapping yarns came to nought. But in the shelter of the tent entrance Bertie managed to cook a meal of noodles on the primus and then made tea using melted snow.

"Well done, Bertie," I said. "Now I expect you to take over the cooking when we get back home."

It was only just after 7 o'clock when Bertie suggested that we get into our sleeping bags in the tent but there seemed no alternative. A radio as well as a bottle of whisky, had been among the items which I had wanted to bring, but Bertie had rejected them as too heavy and not essential. Both of those would have helped pass the time.

"There's lots of time for you to tell me stories, Jake, until it's our usual bed time."

"Okay but you must tell a story too for every story I tell. Now

I've already told the story of how we got to be tucked up in our sleeping bags on snowy Bear Mountain at 7 o'clock on New Year's Eve, so now you can tell the story of the rest of our camping trip."

"OK then, Jake. I'll try but I can't tell stories as well as you."

*****

It was a dark and stormy night, but me and Jake were tucked up snug and warm in our tent and I was feeling really great, especially after Jake liked the dinner I cooked. We were alone, just the two of us out on the mountain with nobody for miles around. I don't think I've ever been so happy since I was wounded. I think I've remembered all the important things and I'm feeling pleased with myself. It's hard for someone like me to remember things and, ever since we decided to go camping, I've been making lists of what it's important not to forget. Writing everything down helps me. I had to hide my lists from Jake because I was afraid it might put him off snow camping. For instance, I wouldn't tell him what the shovel was for. He hadn't asked about the rope but when I used it to tie our food bag high up in a tree, he asked me why. When I explained that it was to keep our provisions away from the bears he looked worried.

So I told him how grizzlies have a good sense of smell and could rip the tent to bits if they thought there was something to eat in there. I know he thought I was a bit crazy because there aren't really any grizzlies in the Park, but I wanted Jake to know that I was doing things properly, the way I had learned to do them when I was on active service.

Jake pretended to look scared, which was nice of him, "Bertie, why didn't you tell me how dangerous this could be? If I'd known that we we'd be in danger of being mauled by grizzlies, I'd never have agreed to come."

43

I told him not to worry because most grizzlies are asleep at this time of year, hibernating. Foxes would be the most likely to go after our food if we left it out.

Jake had to admit that, much to his surprise, he wasn't at all cold or hungry. Of course we were still wearing all our clothes, except our coats which we spread over the sleeping bags as an extra layer to keep us warm. I had remembered to tell Jake that he must keep his hat on because a lot of body heat escapes from your head and he did look funny, lying there with his woolly hat with a pompom at a jaunty angle on top.

But something was niggling me. I felt that there was something very important that I had missed, and I needed to remember what it was to remember what it was before we went to sleep. Here, I was the one in charge for once as it was clear that Jake really knew next to nothing about winter camping. It was up to me to make sure that everything was done properly.

I looked around our tent. By now the moon had come up and its light filtered through the canvas walls of our tent, so it was bright enough for me to see without using the torch. Because of the reflection from all the whiteness of the snow, it was never really completely dark even when clouds covered the moon. Everything looked as it should; the canvas was nice and taut. In the little 'tidy pocket' was our wash-kit, the torch and Jake's bible, which he took everywhere with him. Jake, always a tidy methodical man, had taken off his boots at the entrance to the tent and made me do the same. Just like at home – we always leave our shoes at the front door when we come in.

Then I remembered what it was that I had forgotten. "Jake," I said, "We can't leave our boots where they are. In the morning they'll be frozen stiff and it will be too difficult to get them on. We must take them into our sleeping bags with us to keep them warm."

"You're joking!" he said.

"No. Come on, Jake. Put your boots into one of the plastic bags and then tuck them down at the foot end of your sleeping bag."

Grumbling a bit, he did as told. We had thought that we might have time for several stories but we were so knackered from the long trek up the mountain with our heavy packs that we soon felt sleepy. After I had told Jake a bit about my life in the army before I was injured and invalided out, and he had told me about his life in Africa, he said that it was time for prayers. That's something Jake would never forget. It doesn't bother me; I just let him get on with it.

The wind did blow all night, but it wasn't too fierce and with our tent set well down in the hole we'd dug, the wind passed over us without tugging the guy ropes and tent pegs loose. We both slept pretty well and the next morning we woke to a clean new world with a fresh covering of powdery snow. I made porridge on the primus for our breakfast and then we broke camp as the sun came up.

Going down the mountain was easier than it had been going up and my rucksack was lighter as we had eaten most of the food which we had carried up 'Bear Mountain'. I think Jake thought I really believed this was Bear Mountain and that there were real bears outside the tent, but of course I didn't! I'm not stupid. We took it easy going down stopping often to look at the views and to drink tea from the thermos. Dave was there at the pre-arranged time and congratulated us on looking so fit and well after a night in the wilds. We were soon back home.

After putting away our camping gear and having supper (cooked by Jake) it was time to talk about our expedition. I wanted to know what Jake felt about it now that he was safely home and whether he would consider ever doing something like that again.

"Well, Bertie. I've seen a side of you that I've never seen before," said Jake. "I never expected that I would be the one depending on you to look after me. But I wouldn't have known what to do on a camping trip in the snow and you knew exactly what to do. And thank you mate, for everything. It's been an experience I'll never forget."

Well, I've never felt so proud and pleased with myself. I was grateful to Jake for trusting me. I'd let him down so often in the past when we had tried to do something new (like going to church) where I hadn't been able to cope. This time he had trusted me. And I think that was very brave of him. The trip had probably needed even more courage for him, than I had needed to go to church and I decided I would to try harder to cope with new situations in the future.

However, there was one question I had to ask, "Does that mean that we can do it again next year, Jake?"

THE VACATION

Moira Newlan

It had taken Sandra days to pack for her vacation. She was out of practice, unused to packing at all after the last few years. Every decision now had to be taken on her own, without advice from or consultation with her husband. Packing involved anticipating every situation, every action, every requirement, which might be encountered over the next ten days. The creams for sun and skin, the pretty sandals and sensible shoes, the cool dresses, warm layers and those in-between, a stylish bag for sight-seeing, but a copious one for hand luggage. Luggage! She fretted over the suitcases. Her husband had always taken the largest, all their needs nestled inside, and often aided by using a hired car. She had to be prudent: the lightest possible, at the sacrifice of choices.

It had now been four years since his death, five since the diagnosis. Then the pandemic had descended, wrapping a cloak of constraint around everyone's lives.

Sandra felt the thrill of excitement bubble through her — she would be travelling again, on her own, as she used to do so many times before she was married. Without the compromising: the waiting around for his perfect photograph, the worry over the right lens, his reluctance to visit those cultural sites that she so loved. The thought produced both guilt and relief in equal measure. Her husband had been a Francophile, always persuading her to explore yet another region of that expansive country. The mountains in both the north and south, the hinterland and wine regions, the glories of Provence, the lakes in the central core. It would be churlish to regret those years, but Sandra had wanted a larger slice of the decision making, and a great deal more of the world. Long haul adventures to the far east, cultural highlights of the great European cities — Madrid and Milan, Seville and Sienna, Venice and Vienna. Now, she feared, there would not be the time, or the energy, to follow those dreams. At least this vacation would be a start, mark a new beginning.

It was time to check in, time to sign in, but, oh, she had forgotten the password. She tried to find it on the computer but couldn't remember where to look for it. She tried two of her usual passwords, but to no avail. Then she pressed the re-set password option. After a few minutes, she checked the in-box. Surprisingly, the airline had not responded. She repeated the sequence and still there was no response, not even in spam. She would just need to ask the assistant to check her in when she arrived. It would be many hours before her flight, for she had planned to stay in one of the airport hotels overnight. When she was much younger, she had often slept at the airport on one of the many benches to catch an early flight, but these days of hyper-vigilance, that was not an option, nor would she wish to do so at her age.

The queue at Customer Information was pleasantly short, and soon she was explaining her predicament, while indicating the negligence on their airline's part. Patiently, the young man explained that, while he could process her request, it would cost £50. Sandra was visibly shocked. Instead, he suggested that he would demonstrate how she could complete the process on her mobile, without needing a password. If she could just step aside for now. She began to panic, these were words she did not wish to hear. These instructions fell into her husband's domain, division of labour had allocated every gadget and technical device to his department. But he was not here. Sandra persevered, the assistant took her phone, pressed some more buttons, completed the last part for her, and showed a small diagram and seat number. He reminded her that she would need to do the same again before her flight home — or he could do so at a modest price. She paid the money happily, terrified of forgetting the process and being stranded on the wrong side. He had taken screen shots of both seats and showed her how to access them.

Sandra felt slightly faint. Once, she could simply turn up with a beaten old passport, a paper ticket, sent in advance or handed over by a travel agent. A rucksack, and a friendly face would be enough to see you through. No prepayments, no specified baggage dimensions, no extra charges at the airport, no priority queues. Nor could she remember any of those tiring queues which formed at the gate the next morning, where passengers were called far earlier than was necessary to wait in-line. It might have helped the airline, but not her older legs.

When she finally arrived at her accommodation, she was tired and hungry. The photocopied maps in the hotel were blurred and too small for her eyes. Maps, she was soon to discover, were becoming obsolete. A few were available in the tourist office, but were no longer issued free of charge. People were using apps on their phones to find their way around. Did a screen compare to a paper map? Sandra thought not; her brain was accustomed to understanding spaces by their relative relationships — the station to the piazza or transport link, the museum to the gardens, the airport to the centre, the city as a larger whole. Was it to do with the pandemic? The pandemic had robbed us of our time, of relationships, of freedom of movement, and now it appeared to have robbed us of paper version alternatives. Her heart sank further when searching for a modest trattoria, close to her hotel, a small illegible black and white square was displayed on the building: the QR code. The small digital square which would reveal the menu, if you know how to download it. Sandra did not, nor did she ever want to either.

Close to tears, she noticed a thick, leather-bound menu being presented to diners in the pavement eating area opposite. She crossed the road feeling old and vulnerable, and very alone. It seemed as if her whole identity was being challenged — the once carefree, adventurous, competent, intelligent woman belonged to the past. Time had slowly, invisibly, drained away the old certainties and familiar gateposts. The years of travelling in France by car or rail and occasional flight, and her husband's particular competence, had masked this imperceptible process.

Now she was confronted with her own inadequacy to cope with the new emerging digital world. It held little interest for her, the old ways were preferable.

She sighed, resigning herself to accepting the need to develop those new, necessary skills, if only for future travelling. Or, she supposed, she could simply source one of those reputable travel companies who organise everything for you with sensible flight times and a person at the end of a helpline. She would pay a great deal more. She would have to relinquish the previous pride she had taken in travelling independently. As the Mediterranean sunshine warmed her skin, she felt a little more optimistic. There was a whole world out there waiting for her. She would just need to adapt and travel differently. She was free to make her own decisions now. There were groups she could join, or she could book a ready-made package to wrap around her own mini adventures.

THE DISINTERMENT

Nicola L C Talbot

'Have you heard they're going to disinter the boy Abe?'

That was the first we heard of it, when the gal June told us over coffee. I only had the one biscuit, in case you're wondering about my diet. And there I was thinking she'd invited us over to show off her new three-piece suite with the matching curtains.

'What?' Brenda said. 'Him as was the husband of the old mawther Alice?'

'Exactly, and we all know as how she buried two others before him. Maybe they ought to be disinterred alonga him.'

'Ain't she in a home now?' I said.

June opened a new pack of Mister what's his name's fancy cookies with the big chocolate chunks. Buy one and get a voucher for a new line in cakes that's about to come out.

'That ain't no surprise. She's probably too embarrassed to show her face round here.'

'Her previous one had quite a send-off, didn't he?' Brenda said. 'The boy Bert with a factory out in Dereham. Six bearers with black silk top hats, he had.

'The boy Abe didn't get none of that, that's for sure,' June said. 'And so the police should be suspicious. Didn't I say at the time there was something fishy about it all?'

I helped myself to another biscuit. Well, alright, so I did say I only had the one, but after that news I had to have to another one on account of the shock of it all.

'Well,' the boy Joe said, 'that's a rum ole dew.'

The next bit of news came while we were at the village shop. There was Marge Patterson trying to serve at both the shop counter and the post office counter when the gal June came in, all of a flummox.

'Have you heard what's happened?' she said. 'The police turned up wearing them blue booties and gloves and white outfits, looking like great big overgrown babes, with a big ole vehicle to take the body away, but the grave digger ain't nowhere to be found.'

Poor Marge dropped the change she was trying to count into Patsy Frobisher's hand when she heard that. She's that superstitious that any talk of graves brings her out in shivers.

'Surely they can get someone else,' I said. That's me all over, always pointing out the obvious to everyone.

'Yes of course they can, but the point is no one's seen Horry since he dug Abe's grave. Clean disappeared, he has.'

'Well,' the boy Joe said, 'that's a rum ole dew.'

By the time a new fella arrived from Norwich with his little yellow digger, there was quite a crowd alongside of the churchyard. Not that we were gawping, mind. Just walking the dog and stopping for a mardle with neighbours, as you do.

That old digger went at that wet ground, scooping up bucketfuls of earth, and finally they hoisted up the coffin.

'That's a poor ole box, ain't it?' the gal June said. 'Reckon that's just MDF. I'm surprised that ain't falling apart under Abe's weight, not wishing to speak ill of the dead.'

'That must be a strong old harness,' I said.

We all expected something grisly when they opened up the coffin, and there was young Les Patterson saying how the worms would've already got in and about gas build up and bodies exploding. He's played too many of them video games, if you ask me.

You should've seen the look on everyone's faces when they realised the coffin was empty. Of course, I'd noticed there weren't no strain on the harness, but no one had paid no attention to me, as usual.

'Well,' the boy Joe said, 'that's a rum ole dew.'

So, for the next few weeks the police scoured the neighbourhood, in barns, dredging rivers and poking into the drainage ditches. We had the EDP round and some fella from the radio. Young Les reckoned Abe had been fed to the pigs. That duzzy friend of his with the nose ring said maybe the mawther Alice had dropped Abe down the well, and Les said she'd have had to have jumped up and down on him to make him fit. The two of them made it an excuse for all kinds of mischief as they climbed over fences and dug up people's gardens. Poor old Marge had all her petunias ruined.

They finally found him, on a CCTV camera no less. In a supermarket in Diss, as right as rain. He'd walked in and got collared by a young mawther dressed up as a fairy promoting Mister what's his name's new fairy cakes with the extra fancy sprinkles, and she was trying to make him eat a piece. And who's hand was he holding at the time? Old Horry the grave digger. Turns out they'd faked his death and run off together after Alice had been sent to a home.

'Well,' the boy Joe said, 'that's a rum ole dew, ain't it?'

PASSAGE TO AMERICA

Patrick Linehan

The Peeler swung self-importantly towards Danny, the leather covered baton bouncing off his left hip. Within reach of his right hand a sleeping piglet of a revolver lay in its snap down holster. Twenty feet away by now, his eyes were pinpricks in the pudding of his face, reflecting the glint of the silver chain that snaked in to his breast pocket and on to the lobe of his police-issue whistle. Danny tried not to shift; he kept his hands rigidly in the pockets of his first ever, great coat and looked straight ahead, feigning a slack expression.

One corner of Danny's mind measured up the Peeler, over six feet high, three feet at the widest. His face carried the white marks that had come with routine quelling of street fighting and pub brawls. His belly fought against his tunic and thick thighs tested the width of his trouser legs. His feet were armoured in heavy police service boots, no doubt with sensible steel toecaps. Danny considered how he could stop him and concluded that his own hob-nailed boot — another unaccustomed luxury from barefoot — to Peeler's crotch would be the most effective connection. In a town of this nature, the Peeler would have gained the expertise to counter approaches from the unfriendly, so fast accurate disablement would be essential if he needed to act.

Ten feet away now. Another three steps and their bodies would collide. And then a baby cried and the girl holding it almost hurled it at Danny and said, "Will you take this awful child from me, Danny Maher, and don't be always letting me do the soothing!"

The Peeler stopped, stumped for a moment. Then he said, "Maher, is it? And there was me thinking 'twas Danny Keely. I was sure your picture graced the odd wall back at the station."

"He's not Danny Keely, Sir," said the girl, "He's had no time for any hobbies only me for these last ten months — still less now."

The Peeler's face creased at the girl's unintended description of robbery as a form of pastime.

"Get off this deck," he said. "Go to your quarters, wherever they are. On second thoughts: where did you get such a good overcoat?"

"Me Mammy bought it for us," babbled the girl, "'twill fit either of us if need be."

"Too sensible your mother is," said the Peeler. "Where you're going it'll only get stolen. Now I know someone who could wear it in safety and pleasure. So you can give it to me for safekeeping. Pick it up the next time you're this way."

Danny measured his kick. The Peeler watched him with a smile as his left hand floated to the baton. His right hand flexed into, and then gently out of a half fist.

"There now, peel off the coat," he said, coaxing, threatening. Danny could see the dawning of thick-lipped anticipation on his lumpen face.

"Come on," said the girl, urgently. "Mammy will be waiting below and you know she's sick. Give him the coat. Won't we be inside all the way across."

The baby was a problem for Danny; if he turned aside to drop it he would show his intent as plainly as if he shouted, "I'm going to boot you in the balls!"

"Hold the baby in one hand", said the girl, as if reading his thoughts, "and take the coat off. Come on, gently now."

Danny threw the baby across the gap between him and the Peeler. "Catch," he said and turning, he ran to the stairs, pounding down two, three steps at a time.

The Peeler did catch the child that by now, was screaming against being volleyed unsupported across the chasms between grown-ups! From the strong hands of the Peeler it was no more than an instant before it was on its way again, this time flipped expertly towards its mother.

The Peeler was on his way to the stairs when the mother was felled in front of him by the impact of the child, c tripping him with her long dress and knocking him breathless against the steel deck. By the time he had gathered himself up, Danny's footfalls, so loud and urgent earlier had faded to nothingness. The world consisted of the baby's screaming, the mother's shrilling and the Peeler's own cursing. Though down, he was not out by any means and grabbed at the baby. The mother held on, deftly slipping her hand between the child and its clothes. With the naked baby she turned to run for her life but the Peeler was quicker than her, stamping emphatically on her dress. The skirt came away under his foot and she ran, in her underclothes, to the knot of passengers who had gathered at the noise. The women quickly enveloped her for protection and decency, the men coming to the fore in curiosity and in defence of one of their own.

"He attacked me," she shrieked and then, turning to the Peeler, she said "I don't want to do anything with you. Go away, oh! Go away, please."

"A fine performance, my dear" said the Peeler, confident that he could yet turn this situation to his advantage. "Now you find me my nice overcoat that I was letting Mr Keely wear and we will say no more about the matter. Come on now."

"I know nobody of that name," she said. "All I know is that you tried to handle me and I wasn't having it. And me with a babe in arms. You're filthy. You are supposed to be protecting us."

She started to cry inconsolably, again.

The tender sounded its siren as notice that all non-travelling personnel should leave the ship within fifteen minutes. The Peeler had no intention of travelling, since he was present only as representative of the police authority of the harbour town. For a moment he looked indecisive then, as one last throw he said, "Look, I can keep this ship in harbour for as long as I want, so get me my coat."

This created consternation among those who now stood about and some began to question him. One decided that it was time to involve the representative of the shipping line and went to find him. When he arrived, he attempted to listen to both sides of the story. The more he heard, the more inclined he was to believe that the Peeler had too much dignity to lose by letting the ship sail; it also struck him that if the Peeler were to be allowed to be overridden in this instance, his superiors could prove difficult on future occasions when the ship docked at this harbour. They could, indeed, instigate long, time-consuming searches on the pretext that they were attempting to prevent contraband being shipped to the New World. Further, if passengers — particularly those from the lower decks — were to get wind that an authority higher, even, than the crew, could be side-stepped, any trouble created by them might not be so easily put down on future voyages.

"We can find you a good quality coat, Sir," he said to the Peeler. "Indeed, I'm sure the captain himself could offer you a spare great-coat, we would be more than happy to remove the braid," he added hurriedly.

"I've no need of a hand-out from your owners," said the Peeler. "The nice heavy tailored coat that Mr Keely was willing to return to me is no more than I want. Now see what you can do and we can all be on our way to wherever we might be going, I'll be generous and give you ten minutes."

It was no more than the agent expected. Saving the Peeler's face was now more important than the overcoat.

"We might not be able to find him in that time," he told the Peeler. "Of course we will do our best, so if you could wai . . . ?"

The Peeler stared him down with a mixture of triumph and thinly veiled pity. He had been right in thinking that schedules and a longer-term reputation for disciplined voyages were of paramount importance to the shipping line.

"I'm in no hurry," he said, with a broad wink. "We're working in your time now. The trouble is that the longer I have to wait, the more I have to be finding myself something worthwhile to do on the ship. So don't be too long, there's a good man."

Danny had, by now, got as far as the third level below decks. In an effort to reduce the sound of his flight, he was carrying the hob-nails which were like lead weights on the feet with which he normally walked barefooted about his daily work on the rich peat soil of his landlord's estate in County Cork. He was boiling with sweat under the unaccustomed weight of the overcoat and the constriction of a collar and tie. He desperately ducked into a doorway, lost his footing, and slid for an interminable and terrifying minute down a shaft which dumped him at the oily feet of a blackened engineer tending to the massive coal boilers of the ship.

A shout of, "Jaysus!" went up as the man raised a flat shovel over Danny's head.

"Hold on," said Danny, winded as he was; "don't be hasty."

"What're you doing here?" asked the fireman, still threatening with the shovel.

Danny decided to confess. "I'm trying to escape the Peeler up top."

"Come on, what did you do? Murder someone?" asked the fireman, the shovel now beginning to descend.

Danny rolled sideways, shouting, "No. No. I did not."

The fireman danced, this time swinging the shovel in an arc to catch him on the side of the head.

Danny rolled behind him shouting, "For God's sake wait."

By now a second fireman had arrived at a run and helped his mate to slam Danny up against a metal bulkhead.

"Don't move!" they said in unison.

"I'm not going to," said Danny. "Just let me talk."

"Talk, then!" said the man with the shovel, "I'm warning you, we want no trouble with the law. What did you do?"

"I refused to give the Peeler me new overcoat."

"You stole it, of course," said the fireman. "Why else would he want it?"

"I did not," said Danny, angry that, as working men, they seemed to be taking the side of the law.

"Calm down, calm down; you surely don't expect us to believe that a Peeler would want to take a coat that belonged to you."

"But that's just what he does want to do," said Danny.

By this time a third man who seemed to be in authority, had arrived on the scene.

"What the blazes is going on here?" he asked. "There am I trying to get a bit o' kip and all you lot can do is tap dance on the feckin' steel floor. Who're you?" he asked, suddenly noticing the interloper.

"Danny Keely —"

"He says that the Peeler wants to take his overcoat," said the man with the shovel.

"I didn't steal it, in case you think I did," Danny pre-empted.

"So why does he want it?"

"Search me," said Danny.

"Which Peeler is it?"

"I don't know the Peelers around here," said Danny. "He looked thick, ugly, and a bit battered — like a man who likes a good fight."

The firemen looked at each other significantly; the one who seemed to be in charge turned towards the stairway.

"Stay here. Don't let him out of your sight," he said, looking at his mates, and started up the steps.

The top deck was buzzing when the charge-hand got there. The Peeler, the regular who cleared the ship on its voyages from the port, was leaning against the rail, talking to the first mate. The fireman recognised him as one of those he had seen the previous evening breaking up a fight in the town between sailors from the ship and the local lads who fancied their chances, and in which he himself had been involved. He had considered himself lucky to escape in the confusion, since he had had to wield a knife in his defence against a superior local brawler. He stepped back into the doorway from which he had come and watched and listened as the women present comforted a screaming girl with a baby. The captain was barking orders at the master-at-arms to search the ship and to bring a thief in his twenties to their deck to hand over a coat which the Peeler wanted to recover. The ship would not sail until the thief and coat had been surrendered.

He took the stairs downwards as quickly as he could, not bothering to hide the noise of his progress. Once he had gone half way down, he calculated the odds against hiding the interloper, who had been cornered by his two mates in the engine room. Might be worth it if the overcoat were up as a trade, all the better if there were to be an additional sweetener of money. He doubted though, that there were any great riches to be had in this instance and thought to hand the fellow over, much though it went against the grain to assist the Peelers in any way. But then, if the captive were not surrendered it was likely that the team of marines, kept on board to ensure good conduct of all and sundry — and that included himself and his men — would come searching. They knew every inch of the ship and once deployed, were ruthless in their methods. He would have to be handed over, and with the coat. He considered which was the more important, the man or the coat, and made a snap decision to give up the coat and hold the man, just in case anything could be gained for himself.

He shot into the engine room at a gallop and shouted, "Get the coat off him. Quick!"

At the sound of his voice the captors were momentarily distracted and Keeley squirmed loose making a desperate dive for the door. The chargehand stuck out a foot snicking the prisoner's ankle just enough to trip him on the turn and send him sprawling and slithering on the steel deck. It was enough to give the crewmen time to hurl themselves on top of him; they bent his head back so that he was looking straight in front of him and began to strip off the coat. He couldn't plead or fight his corner for he was unable to breathe through a windpipe flattened against his gullet; he could only give out gargling sounds as they cursed their way to ridding him of the coat.

Then he found himself being lifted and slammed down hard against what seemed like the floor of a storage bin and before the lid was shut, one of the firemen grated, "Keep your mouth shut if you don't want to be handed over to that Peeler. Once you go up the stairs, you're unlikely to see the outside of a prison for years. So shut up!"

Fury boiled up in him and his immediate reaction was to attempt to lever the bin's lid upwards. But having been weakened by the preceding struggle and now half smothered by coal dust, he decided to give up the struggle at least temporarily. It seemed that someone was sitting on the lid in any case before he heard the bolt being shot home.

The chargehand had the coat and was, with slow deliberation, heading up the stairs. At the level below the fracas and planning to create a false scent, he made a detour to ensure that he came up by the stairs farthest away from the one he guessed that Danny had descended. As he approached the final flight, he met a cabin boy doing his rounds.

"What's going on upstairs?" he asked.

"Something about a stolen overcoat." said the lad.

"Funny," he said. "I came across this just along the corridor. Ask them if this is it."

The lad was eager to oblige and trotted up to the captain, who had arrived on the scene. He waited while the officer finished a further offer of a coat to the Peeler.

"Beg pardon Sir," he said, "This was found below deck. What shall I do with it?"

"That's my coat," roared the Peeler, as much in relief as in righteous indignation for truth to tell, the situation was beginning to slip from his grasp. "Just as I described it. Give it here, young man".

"Just a moment," said the captain. "I thought you said that one of my passengers had run off in it?"

"Well, yes;" said the Peeler. "But now that I have my coat back, I won't be over hard on you and your passengers. I'm sure that you have the authority to deal with any dishonesty that you might find on board if I leave you to get on your way immediately. After all, it isn't as if any criminal can escape from the ship once you set sail, now, is it?"

"So, you want me to ship criminals to America, then, do you?" asked the captain, angrily. "How do you think that would stand with my own reputation and the reputation of our Shipping Line. Indeed, how do I know that the next time I pass this way one of you Peelers won't hold the ship up, just as you are doing now? I think we had better find your criminal and let you take him along with the coat."

"No. No," said the Peeler. "I didn't mean criminal as such. After all, the young man only forgot to give me back the coat I lent him to keep the baby warm. There now, I think we can all be on our way. The tender is alongside so I'll be off. Have a good trip, Captain; we'll see you next time you come this way."

"Well, we have enough people to witness this state of affairs," said the Captain. "I do believe that we all have important business to attend to so we'll call it a day for now. Do be careful as you bridge the gap to the tender, won't you. Hope to see you next time around."

"Thank you," said the Peeler. "Always a pleasure doing business with a gentleman."

"Indeed it is," said the Captain, deadpan. "Goodbye to you."

"Goodbye," said the Peeler.

The irony of their last remarks was lost on neither of them. Any relationship they might have was founded on their mutual self-interest and owed nothing to either gentility or good manners.

Down in the boiler room the dust was settling in the bin where Danny lay, quieter now in his own interests. He could hear the engineers and stokers moving around the floor outside his box and, presently, felt the greater movement of the ship. This was unaccustomed motion – he had never before even set eyes on the sea let alone travelled on its surface.

The Voyage to America was under way.

MUDDY BOOTS

Shirley Buxton

'Why do I have to keep telling you over and over again not to walk through the house in your muddy boots? I'm fed up with having to mop the floor every time you come in.'

As always, Mum's rant fell on deaf ears, as Josh blocked his mother's words. Not stopping, he headed straight out of the back door into the garden. Dropping his bag by the wood pile, he made for the compost heap to relieve himself. It had on the whole been a good day and now he felt safe on home territory.

Life had certainly taken a positive turn when his college had arranged a placement with Robbie. Landscape gardening was, of course, a perfect match for someone infatuated with soil and digging. As a small child Josh had been fascinated by the worms and centipedes he dug up. Now his shelves were full of books not just for the identification of a myriad of mini-beasts, but about soil types and its composition. With encouragement from his grandfather, Josh had extended his interest to plants. He could tell anyone who had the patience to listen, what would grow well in any type of soil but tended to lose their interest as he launched into detailed explanations about pH testing. Robbie could see the potential in this rather unusual young man. College and Josh were not a good match. Robbie arranged to take Josh on as an apprentice and even succeeded in convincing the college authorities that day release was not necessary. Robbie assured them that he could include most elements of their basic English and maths curriculum into the apprenticeship programme. He could see that Josh's problems were not academic but with the institution.

Josh thrived. School hadn't worked for him, neither had College. He'd found the other students difficult. He was taunted by the boys and laughed at by the girls. His surname Thorne seemed to cause great mirth. He hated the name-calling. At first it was Thorny, then Spiky, later Spineless and Pointless. When he'd gone to work with Robbie there was another Josh so he'd been asked if he had a nickname. That was a most difficult day and Josh thought of walking out. Fortunately, Robbie was a good boss who quickly picked up on the problem and dealt with the situation. He couldn't understand when the other Josh, Josh White, happily agreed to be called Chalky.

The best bit about this job and his new friends was that nobody minded his boots. Boots were the only footwear Josh tolerated; wellington boots when he was small, progressing through Doc Martins to workman's steel caps. In this line of work everyone wore boots and all of them were just as muddy as his.

This particular evening, he was in a pensive mood. He was trying to make sense of what had happened during the day. He had experienced a number of feelings that were new to him. It had been late in the afternoon when Helen, who had commissioned their latest landscaping project, had bought her daughter Rosie to see the transformation of the grounds. Josh immediately understood the look of shock on Rosie's face. This was unusual feeling number one. He'd been told he lacked empathy, but just this once he had understood. Rosie's reaction was surely natural when seeing such a dramatic change to the garden that you had played in and enjoyed since you were a small child. Helen and Robbie seemed dismayed by Rosie's lack of appreciation. Having achieved good grades at school, she was now studying botany at university. Helen had assumed her daughter would be pleased and excited by what they had achieved! They plied her with explanations about the changes and further plans for the garden until, to their surprise, Rosie just ran off. Josh however understood the pain and confusion that could be caused by change.

He had found her later on a bench near the untouched end of the garden. This resulted in unusual feeling number two: Josh felt a connection with this girl and, more than that, a feeling of warmth. He sat on the far end of the bench and waited. It seemed an age until she looked up. For once he didn't instinctively look away but held her gaze before saying

'I know. I'm sorry.'

She cried on his shoulder. He held her and comforted her, just in the way that his mother had held him on the numerous occasions when his world had dissolved into chaos.

Then there was strange feeling number three: they had kissed. It was his first romantic kiss, and it happened so naturally. It was a kiss of understanding, thanks, respect, acceptance and kinship. It shot through his body bringing him alive, it excited him and he didn't want it to stop. Rosie clung to him until the magic was broken by the sound of footsteps heading their way.

That afternoon had changed him. Perhaps he'd 'grown up'. Whatever had happened that day, Josh knew that he and Rosie understood each other. She made him feel good, in fact happier and more certain of himself than he'd ever felt before.

I WAS A STRANGER

Stuart McCarthy

The Brigadier sat in the stern and prayed the searchlights wouldn't find them. The Germans had been looking for him for the months of his convalescence but the sisters, in whose house he stayed, had made sure that Jens Toordstra would not be found. Following his escape from hospital they had tended his wound, fed him and kept him safe until he was well enough to make his way through the lines to his own side. He owed his life to these quietly heroic people who had welcomed him, a stranger, into their home.

In the front of the boat Pieter van Elft rowed steadily and silently. Pieter was the one who had got him out of the hospital just before his transfer to Germany, who had talked with him throughout those long months and had given him the name Jens Toordstra, a labourer from Rotterdam. That was the name they had used on the occasions when German patrols came by looking for allied servicemen left behind when the paratroops retreated.

'Your people will be waiting for us on the bank,' said Pieter quietly, 'you will get out and I will row back. We shall not meet again, which is a sadness for me, I have enjoyed our talks.'

The boat ground to a halt on the shingle and the Brigadier jumped out. He turned and shook Pieter by the hand.

'Farewell my friend, until the next time,' said Hackett and he turned and scrambled up the bank.

'Brigadier Hackett,' said the young lieutenant who was waiting, 'welcome back.'

It was then that the night was riven by searchlight beams, the sound of gunfire and shattering wood. The lights showed the remnants of a boat.

'Looks like your transport has bought it,' said the officer, 'pity, but these things do happen.' He looked with disdain at Hackett's torn and stained clothing, 'If you would like to follow me you will want to freshen up and change before the General meets with you.'

That afternoon his commander was waiting in his well-appointed office and held out his hand in friendship.

'John, it is good to see you. We thought you'd been killed.'

Hackett shook his hand and smiled, 'I was wounded, but a German surgeon operated and saved my life. They were going to take me to Germany but the resistance got me away and hid me. They nursed me back to health and got me out. I owe them a lot. I was a stranger and they took me in. Now I have a month's-worth of questions starting with what happened?'

'How do you mean?'

'I mean, how did it happen that we were landed some eight hours late and the Germans were waiting for us? How did it happen that none of our radios worked? How did it happen that none of the promised transport was there and how did it happen that we were not supported as promised?'

The General looked at him as if were an idiotic schoolboy, 'Weather and a logistical difficulty that was addressed in the following days.'

'By which time,' responded the Brigadier angrily, 'I lost nearly two thirds of my men, killed or wounded, and Arnhem Bridge is still in German hands. I think you'll have to do better than that.'

'Gavin's Americans couldn't get there in time. They found the job to be one bridge too far for them.'

'And why was that?'

'The road was one lane. If a tank broke down the others couldn't get past. The Germans knew this and were very busy.'

'And this wasn't thought of at the planning stage?'

'It was, but was discounted.'

'And 4th Brigade suffered for it.'

The Brigadier stood at the window looking out over the valley, which his troops had fought so hard for and would have to go back and fight all over again. 'Where are they? I want to see them, to let them know I'm alive.'

'They were disbanded. It was felt better for morale if they were spread around other units. Better all round.'

Hackett turned and faced his commanding officer, his eyes as bleak as the wind from Siberia. 'Get them together. When Arnhem is liberated I want to lead them in. They deserve no less.'

The General went white, his lips compressed into a .tight line. 'Very well Brigadier, you shall have your wish but be very careful how you act in future. The army, the country, they come first, last and all the time. We cannot have individual commanders who can't possibly see the bigger picture dictating policy to Command. I am sorry for the loss of your Brigade but these things happen in war. Now, if you will excuse me, I have a meeting with Monty to discuss future strategy. Your name will surely come up. I will pass on your, — attitudes to him. Good day Brigadier.'

The General picked up his cap and gloves and left the room leaving Hackett to his thoughts.

The assault on Arnhem was better planned and largely successful. The bridge, however, had to be rebuilt; the American air force had destroyed it to prevent the Germans bringing up reinforcements. Hackett wondered anew just what the point of it all was, but put such thoughts to one side as he prepared the remnants of the 4th. Parachute brigade for its entry into Arnhem.

He marched with them as they made their way through the streets. At a familiar road junction, he left the main body and went alone to a house he knew well. He knocked on the door and was greeted by the two sisters, and to his joy and delight by Pieter van Elft.

'Pieter, you made it,' he said, 'I thought for all the world you'd died when the boat was fired on.'

'I jumped and swam, I was lucky,' answered Pieter. 'You are looking well.'

They hugged then, and Hackett handed out his gifts of food and cheeses. Pieter accepted them with tears in his eyes.

'So, Jens Toordstra is a Tommy,' he said.

SAM AND THE LITTLE BLUE BOAT

Alison Court

The day was hot, again. It was the first day of their summer holiday, and John and Jim were to spend a happy outdoors morning with their chestnut, floppy-eared dog Sam. They sprang out of bed even earlier than on school days, in their eagerness to play in the beauty of the day. They threw on their clothes and ran off across the fields towards the river.

All morning they romped in the fields and on the riverbank, throwing clods of earth into the river, so that Sam would paddle wildly to the widening circles . . . to find . . . what? He swam and swam, and was puzzled every time.

John and Jim stripped off their shorts and shirts and thrashed around in the water. They tied twine they found in the hedgerow onto hazel twigs and fished in vain for their lunch.

The sun was high by now, so it must have been around midday when they realised they were hungry. They looked around; they were a long way from home, far upstream beyond the bridge at Lechlade. It would take ages to get home from here.

All three set off running, but soon they came across something they hadn't spotted before, hidden under the riverbank bushes — a little blue rowing boat, complete with oars.

John looked at Jim; Jim looked at John; a light went on in both their heads. As one, they leapt off the bank onto the cracked and dried shore, and pulled the boat out from its hiding place. Sam leapt in from the bank, the boys turned the boat to head downstream and pushed, as they too both leapt.

But they both missed. John tripped over a submerged branch, and Jim tripped over John. They fell into the water, splashing and thrashing and laughing, but when they got to their feet, what a shock — for there was Sam sailing downstream in the little blue boat, already out of reach.

They were stunned. What should they do? They clambered back up the bank and started to run, to try to catch up with the little blue boat that was picking up speed as it headed towards Lechlade and beyond.

They lost time at gates with difficult latches and again with undone shoelaces. The little boat was in the distance now, Sam standing at the stern looking beseechingly back towards them.

And so their paths diverged. The little blue boat carried on its way, Sam now standing at the bow, watching the world unfold before him, as the boys headed home for help.

Hours passed. All afternoon, the little boat floated down the river, past fields and woods, under bridges. Sam hid from the hot sun under the rear bench, so that the only two walkers on the riverbank, in the whole of that hot afternoon, did not see a little dog adrift.

At last the heat of the day receded a little, as the little boat approached a city dotted with distant golden towers — Oxford.

People in houseboats and on the riverbank were reappearing; it felt like the start of the day, even though the sun was on its way down.

Sam woke and stood on the bench in the middle of the boat, looking at the swelling crowds of tourists on the riverbank. He was thirsty by now and panting. The tourists waved and called to him before raising their cameras to capture the image of a little dog on a little blue rowing boat.

At Christ Church Meadow, hordes of young people and families were picnicking and playing games. But no one rescued Sam and he sailed ever onwards downstream.

Later, after Clifton Hampden, there was a last gaggle of children swimming and jumping in the water, laughing, splashing, having fun, but the river was moving fast and even they, fearless as they were, dared not swim so far into the current to try to rescue the little dog. He sailed on.

And thus he sailed overnight, all night, past settlements small and large, following the meanders in the river between field, outcrops, woods.

Sam tucked himself down onto the bottom boards and slept most of the night. At least that took his mind off being thirsty. He was anxious but he trusted that he would be saved in the end; he knew from his happy home that humans put things right.

Early morning and the little boat seemed to change direction constantly, as the river wound its way between steeply wooded hills.

Suddenly, there was a disparate group of dishevelled men, and beautiful women in long, sparkly, swirling dresses and high heels, the end of an all-night affair. Some of them held champagne glasses aloft and they lurched and tottered in a haphazard way along the path.

"DaAHling, look at the little dog, he's so sweet!" called one of the young women, and they turned their bleary eyes Sam-wards. Sam, his tongue hanging out, looked at them contemptuously, for he knew they would not be forthcoming in rescue plans.

All morning the little boat sailed on and still there was no rescue in sight. Dog walkers, hikers, families on the riverbank were so surprised to see a little dog at the prow of a little blue rowing boat that they could only turn and stare. Some of them wondered if they were hallucinating, as the sun rose higher on yet another hot day.

It must have been early afternoon, and the little boat was well on its way into London past magnificent palaces and street upon street of comfortable houses.

Sam was panicking now. All his life he had been surrounded by a loving family, looking after him every minute of the day, and now he was alone in the wide world and no one cared, no one noticed him. His little heart started to thump anxiously as he sailed ever more rapidly downstream.

At the end of the afternoon, he drifted past Big Ben and the Houses of Parliament, and the great wheel in the sky. There were thousands of people on the riverbank, with cameras and ice creams, looking around and having fun. There was so much happening on the river, with pleasure boats cruising up and down, that one little blue rowing boat scarcely seemed to attract anyone's attention, even though there was a little chestnut dog in it, letting out an occasional but increasingly frantic bark.

The river was becoming ever wider, there were more big boats on the river and big buildings on the riverbank, and fewer people to be seen. Sam ran up and down, desperately looking to see from where help might come. This part of the river was scarier than before.

And still the river meandered in great bends and loops; it was so disorientating.

Sam was starting to lose heart altogether. It was evening again, he was lost, he was hungry and thirsty. He didn't want to spend another dark night in the bottom of the boat. He was scared.

Ahead of him the river was broadening out. Dilapidated old buildings stood on the riverbank and then great towers of flats, some new and flashy, others old and brown. People were specks in the distance.

A blast of a horn blew from a great ferry over on the left, and, shortly, the ferry left the pierhead and started to turn in the river before heading to the opposite shore.

The little boat started to rock from side to side, caught in the slip of the big ferry. It swung to the left, then to the right, up and down, faster and faster. Sam held on tight and struggled to keep his balance. He was sure he was going to fall into the water, and then what would become of him? He was more scared than ever.

But suddenly, he pricked up his ears. Above all the noise of the horn and the engines, he thought he could hear the sound of voices he knew?

"Sam, Sam, Sam, we're here. Sam, look, we're here." And suddenly, there they were, frantically waving, leaning over the railings on the huge ferry.

And over there, on a river-police boat that was rapidly heading towards the little blue boat, there were the boys' mother and father. "Sam," they called, "stay there, Sam, we're coming."

The police boat circled Sam in his little blue boat and headed him off so he could travel no further into the wake of the ferry. The policeman hooked a ladder over the side of his launch, climbed down, scooped Sam into his arms, and climbed back up.

Sam was beside himself. He was rescued, he was safe. Excitedly, he licked the policeman's face all over. But the policeman, happy though he was to be licked with such fervour, knew that Sam must be parched, and he extracted himself and duly presented the happy dog with a large trough, filled to the brim with water. Sam lapped it up, every drop.

They chugged happily back to the Woolwich pier, where the ferry was docking. Jim and John were the first off the boat, the ferrymen cheering loudly behind them.

They ran, as fast as their legs could carry them, to the police boat and to their beloved dog Sam. The happy sounds of their reunion rang up and down the river for a long time.

That was the happiest of happy summer evenings.

And still, the rest of the summer lay ahead.

ARCTIC EXPEDITION
Avril Suddaby

From the journal of a member of the 1937 expedition to the Arctic

Spitzbergen   02.00 hours   20 July, 1937

My companions have retired for the night but I know that I won't be able to get to sleep. I am too excited. It's our last night on board the Isbjorn, and tomorrow we'll disembark on the northern-most part of Spitzbergen. After the crew have helped us unload our equipment, they'll set off back to Tromso as quickly as possible to get the rest of our supplies and bring them to us. Speed is essential before the ice grips the Arctic in its deadly embrace, from which there is no escape.

We left Tromso, 300 miles north of the Arctic Circle, just over a week ago. We, that is myself and my four colleagues – comprise a team which is to carry out a scientific survey of this part of the Arctic, where we will spend the coming winter. I am responsible for communications, for setting up the equipment – receivers, transmitters, wireless mast and generator, and for sending three weather reports a day to London.

Naturally, I am apprehensive. At present we are experiencing the white nights, almost 24 hours of daylight with an ever-decreasing brief interval of twilight. And we are moving relentlessly toward total darkness when, for months, the sun will never rise above the horizon. How will I cope?

I have read about 'rar', which can make men go mad. The nearest English translation is cabin fever.

There will be times when blizzards will rage day after day and it would be madness to step outside of our cabin into the darkness and howling winds which can blow a man off his feet. The food will be monotonous. How will I manage the tension caused by living in an enclosed cramped space, where the personal habits of others can so easily become more than just everyday irritations.

But that lies ahead. For now I am delighting in this brief Arctic summer of eternal daylight. It is nothing like what I had thought it would be. I had imagined the Arctic as vast, white, silent, barren and devoid of life. As we progressed up the coast of Spitzbergen I learned how wrong I had been!

First, about the colours, I had thought everything would be blindingly white, I had not expected the eerie blue and mauve colours of the ice. Secondly, the noise. There is an endless cacophony of shrieking birds, mainly seagulls. And the ice makes weird creaks and groans as if it is talking to itself. Every now and then there is a dramatic explosion as a part of a glacier breaks away and crashes into the sea.

The wild life is amazing; I've seen puffins, Arctic foxes, herds of reindeer, walruses and seals on the ice floes, and even a glimpse of a polar bear with her cub. The animals are living life to the full, making the most of this short summer. All this I wouldn't have missed for anything.

After the Isbjorn has delivered the rest of our supplies and leaves us, we'll be alone, only the five of us during the long winter months until the sun returns and the ice eventually retreats far enough that ships can reach us.

Although apprehensive I am optimistic. I am resolved to be strong and to overcome the difficulties. I will carry out my part in the work of this expedition to the best of my ability. I hope, and must believe that we will all come out stronger from the trials which we endure together.

To find out more about this expedition to the Arctic and what might have happened to the members of the party, you should read Michelle Paver's Dark Matter, *which was the inspiration for this fictitious journal. Published in the UK by Orion Publishing Group (2010).*

THE DECISION
Moira Newlan

If music be the food of love, play on! proclaimed Harrison Harvey, delighted by his clever quotation, unusual for this man, though its origin was beyond him. His youngest child Olivia was practicing the cello before her grade exams, while his wife toiled in the kitchen preparing Sunday lunch. Lacking social skills and a good education, Harvey had managed to build a highly successful business through rigorous application and ruthless management. He had taken opportunistic risks, been lucky, and now owned a two-million-pound property in the leafy Home Counties, plus several less valuable, elsewhere, earning him a lucrative portfolio income.

Simon looked at his father and turned indulgently towards him. Inwardly, however, he felt confused, dissatisfied, and restless. He had been working for an NGO in a country recovering from decades of war and conflict. After a year of service, staff were allowed one visit back home. Here he was now, in his family house in this affluent, luxurious, sanitised sanctuary, this repository of worldly goods, unnecessary new gadgets, overstuffed cupboards and fridges and free flowing alcohol. Here on the table, lay his mother's magazines covering the latest, smartest fashions, beauty tips, interior design ideas, garden make-over options, and brochures for cars and holidays. All seemed trivial and irrelevant. He felt detached and disgusted. Maybe this was how soldiers used to feel while on home leave from the trenches, unable to reconcile those two opposing worlds, these dual realities.

He owed all his expensive education and opportunities to his father. Yet, in that moment, he despised this self-satisfied, arrogant man. This man who stubbornly believed that a rich life could be gained by hard work alone and measured solely in terms of acquired worldly goods. How simplistic and ignorant a view. Simon's announcement that he had accepted a position with an NGO in Indo-China, had been met with surprise and disappointment, as he had anticipated.

Wasting your education and your degree.

When I was your age, I was already earning . . .

I'm sure your brothers could find you something in their organisations.

His mother had been less judgemental, concerned more for his safety and welfare in such, to her, an unknown part of the world. Her other children had sailed seamlessly into their careers, while Olivia, by far the brightest, was applying to Oxford to study for a Law degree. Simon, she knew, had never known what to do or which direction to take. He had been a good 'allrounder', passed all his exams adequately but had never demonstrated any passion or special aptitude for any single subject. His decision to take time out had made perfect sense to her.

Simon's new world had opened up to him in layers. The first few weeks had been spent slowly adjusting to the heat, the dust, the rhythms of the new location, as well as all those expectations and challenges of his new employment. Then gradually, he began to form new friendships, not just with other Western colleagues, but also with the local men and women. The country had a young population. A whole generation of parents and grandparents had either perished or been traumatised during its turbulent recent history. The youngsters were eager to hear about Simon's life, happy to practice their English and to share gossip and friendships. The basic simplicity of his domestic arrangements had at first been quite a shock, but he soon began to appreciate this less wasteful way of living:

- a banana leaf served as a plate

- a coconut fully used: the refreshing juice for drinking, the white creamy flesh for cooking, the shell for a flowerpot or turned into a bowl

- hats, bags, and baskets woven from local reeds and barks

- water sufficient but not wasted on dishwashers or flushing toilets.

Transport was cheap and plentiful, to accommodate all budgets. Bicycles, mopeds, small motorbikes or tuk-tuks served the population well, often piled high with families, food, furniture or anything else considered portable. The more affluent did drive imported cars, but they looked out of place on the narrow roads and broken surfaces, proving a menace to other transport forms. Simon thought of his father's SUV parked on the driveway, his mother's sporty 'run-around' Audi, and the metallic lines of driver-only cars, with empty seats and boots, commuting daily to work along the M25 corridor and every arterial route to the capital.

With time, Simon's work as an 'Eco tourism Development Officer' became more rewarding. It involved helping to build capacity among the locals and persuading them that this new source of income would be more profitable and sustainable than fishing already depleted stocks or logging the disappearing forests. Instead, homestays, small restaurants, local craft shops, and specialised tours could be established, the potential was huge. The community had been surprised that tourists would travel from far-away countries to visit their land or show interest in their way of life. Gradually, though, they, too, noticed which features drew the tourists to their habitat – the rare wildlife, and particular plant species, unique areas of semi-submerged woodland and the local ecosystems. They began to delight in this new appreciation. Despite their poverty, Simon observed, people were often smiling and friendly and happy to help. It was a quality not lost on travellers and proved infectious.

Maria called out from the kitchen that lunch was ready.

Well my boy, good to have you home again! his father's strident voice boomed out. *I suppose you'll go back to that godforsaken place and finish your contract? In my opinion, you'd be better to quit now and get on with real life here. You've had your gap-year.*

Using all his newly acquired skills of patience and diplomacy, Simon suppressed his anger and replied quietly, *Actually Dad, it's really interesting work and useful. It's making a difference to people's lives. Why don't you and Mum come over and visit? There are some pretty decent hotels in the area now and you could see for yourselves?'*

He wanted to add that it was also a much more religious nation than their own and maybe that was why everyone was so kind and helpful but he knew it would be futile.

Yes, yes, we'll think about it. What we really want to know is what your intentions are when you do finally return?

Oh, that's easy, Dad! I've decided to join the Charity Sector and do something useful. I know I'll never earn very much but my ideas of what's sufficient have change, and are very different from yours, I expect. I'm very clear about my direction and I'd appreciate it if the whole family would accept my decision.

Before her father could catch his breath, Olivia interjected quickly, *Good on you Simon. It takes courage to stand up for what you believe in, and we all admire courage and vision, don't we Dad? Mum? Mmm ... what's that Shakespeare quotation from Macbeth? 'Who could refrain that had a heart to love and in that heart, courage to make love known?'*

THE BRIEFCASE

Nicola L C Talbot

(Reprint of an e-book short story published by Dickimaw Books.)

Aide had met Annie at their local film club fifteen years ago. Her smile had been the first thing he'd noticed about her, and the little lopsided dimples in her cheeks. She'd been full of fun and laughter. They'd married and toured the Oxford Canal for their honeymoon.

When had things started to go wrong? It was her job, he was sure of it. It was all quite stupid, really. She was just a secretary to some kind of tech company. Although from the way she acted, you'd think it was something far more important. Why should she feel under pressure when all she had to do was file documents?

First, she'd had to take overtime, and then there were the business trips, but she never said much about what she was doing. Why the secrecy?

'I've signed a confidentiality agreement,' Annie said. 'I'm not allowed to talk about work.'

'I thought you trusted me.'

'I trust you not to hurt or betray me.'

'No, you don't. If you did, you'd know I wouldn't disclose anything confidential.'

'I'm not allowed to discuss work.'

It was just an excuse, but two could play at that. He wouldn't say anything about his work, either. That would teach her. So, a few days later, he came home from work and heaved a sigh.

'Things are really hairy at work,' he said. 'It's so stressful.'

'D'you want to talk about it?'

'I can't. It's confidential.'

'Okay. I understand.'

She gave him a hug, but he was too angry to reciprocate.

'How about we go out to the cinema on Friday?' she said.

'Can't. Have to work overtime. In fact, I'm going to have to go in on Saturday as well.'

He didn't really, but she'd been working overtime so much lately that it was her turn to stay home alone. He'd go to the pub, and it'd serve her right.

'Oh, okay,' she said. 'I'd turned down a request to go away this weekend, but since you're working, I may as well take the assignment.'

Assignment? She made it sound like she was some kind of secret agent. What type of secretary goes on assignments?

'Whatever,' he said.

On Friday night, he slumped down on a bar stool with a pint of beer. The place was crowded and smelt of body odour, alcohol, and salt and vinegar infused furniture polish. A big screen on one wall was showing the news, but no one was paying any attention to it, and it couldn't be heard above the noise of people talking and laughing, with occasional shrieks as a glass was spilt.

A young woman squeezed into the gap next to Aide and tried to attract the barman's attention. She had long black hair tied in two braids, thick black eyeliner with what must be false eyelashes sweeping up in a point, matching the eyeliner beneath, and was wearing a black miniskirt, over-the-knee black socks with rubber-soled black boots, and long black opera gloves. The only thing she was wearing that wasn't black was bright red lipstick.

The barman came over. She ordered a shandy, glanced at Aide as she turned round, gave a friendly smile, and then squeezed her way through the crowd. He lost sight of her, but caught glimpses of her pale face with crimson lips from time-to-time until last orders rang.

She was there again the next evening. She gave Aide a casual smile and was once again lost in the crowd. She looked the kind of person who smiled at everyone. A goth with a sunny disposition.

On Sunday, he decided he couldn't be bothered to cook for himself and went to have lunch at the pub. The television was now showing a rugby match, which he settled down to watch, cheering and groaning along with his fellow patrons. The elation of a perfect try had to be shared and, as he looked around the sea of joyful faces, he saw the goth girl, her smile now a beaming grin.

At the end of the match, everyone crowded around the bar for a refill, and the after-match discussions led to small groups forming and rearranging until he found himself talking to her about certain changes that had been made to the regulations, and whether or not they had improved the game.

It was a friendly chat. Nothing else. They happened to meet again after that, but just as acquaintances: regulars of the same pub who talked about sport.

'I'm Aide, by the way.'

'I'm Lucy.'

That was all the personal information they shared. He didn't inquire further. He didn't want her to feel he was coming on to her. They celebrated rugby victories and commiserated over defeats, and laughed about trivia.

But one day her sunny disposition had clouded over.

'What's up?' he asked.

'Oh, stuff,' she shrugged. 'Found out my partner was cheating on me.'

'That's rotten.'

'Should've guessed, really. Too many excuses. Know what I mean?'

'Yeah. I know.'

'Anyway. I'll be alright. Better off without him.'

Too many excuses. Yeah, he knew that one. Overtime. Trips away. Secrets. Why all the secrets? It wasn't like she was working for MI5. Confidentiality agreement. Who did she think he'd tell, anyway? Probably just a load of business management crap. Who gives a damn about it?

He hadn't meant to say anything to Lucy about it, but somehow it all came out while they drank.

'D'you know how I found out?' Lucy said. 'It was in his briefcase. "Just work documents, love." That's what he used to say.'

'That's what Annie says, as well. Keeps it locked up.'

'Load of bull. It was in amongst a pile of boring old documents. Just work documents, my arse.'

'What d'you find?' he asked.

'Don't know if I should talk about it.'

They drank some more for a while.

'Hotel reservations,' she said. 'Honeymoon suite.'

'Could it have been a surprise?' Aide said. 'You know, maybe he was planning a trip for you both?'

'The booking date was for the previous weekend. While he was away on a work trip. And there was an opened packet of condoms.'

'Oh. That's bad.'

Somehow the revelation of Lucy's partner's infidelity seemed to doom his own relationship. If it could happen in Lucy's case, then surely it could happen for him too? Would he also find the same kind of evidence?

'But anyway,' he said, as though he'd been discussing his thoughts out loud, 'I don't have the key to her briefcase. She never leaves it lying around.'

'I'll tell you something –' Lucy glanced round and leaned towards him '– but I shouldn't really say. I got in with a bad lot for a while in college. Had this boyfriend who taught me how to unpick locks. His dad was a con. He learnt it off him. I've still got the gear. Well, he's not coming back for it, anyway. I'm straight now, but that's how I unlocked it.'

A few pints more, and the decision was made. It had to be a time when Annie's briefcase was home but she wasn't. That didn't happen very often, except for when she went to Pilates on a Wednesday. They'd do it then.

In the cold, sober light of day, Aide wondered if he was doing the right thing, but it wasn't like he was planning any kind of romantic evening with Lucy. He didn't fancy her. She was just a friend. A mate from the pub. They weren't going to get up to anything — apart from pick the lock on his wife's briefcase to search for incriminating information. It was her own fault for being so secretive, for not trusting him. If they found nothing, everything would be alright.

Wednesday evening finally came along. No overtime tonight. After dinner, Annie went off to Pilates as usual. Lucy turned up ten minutes later at the back door in her black miniskirt and long black gloves, with a pronounced cleavage showing above a front-laced leather corset. Would anyone really believe she was just a mate from the pub sneaking into his house?

91

'D'you think this is right?' Aide said. 'I mean, I'm not sure about this.'

'It's okay. No harm done, if there's nothing there, and, if there is, then she's the one who should be feeling guilty, right?'

'Right.'

But he stood there, staring at her — trying not to stare at the bow of her laces nestled in the gap between her breasts.

'You know,' she said, 'now the initial shock is over, I'm glad I found out. We weren't getting along. I was just kidding myself things were okay. I'm not in denial about it anymore.'

'Yeah, you're right. Let's do it.'

'Maybe you should keep watch,' she said, 'and I'll take a look. That way if there's nothing there, you can honestly say you never peeked.'

'Okay.' It was certainly the easiest solution, but what if there were confidential documents? What if there was cash inside and Lucy filched it? With her iffy background, a large amount might be too tempting for her. 'No. No, I'd better stay with you.'

'Suit yourself.'

He found the briefcase, and Lucy deftly unpicked it, while he stood next to her, breathing in the faint scent of coconut from her hair. The locks clicked and she eased open the case. It contained sheets of paper with strange symbols and diagrams. No hotel reservation, no packets of contraceptives or other signs of a liaison.

'Is that someone coming up the path?' Lucy said, looking up sharply.

Confident now that there was no cash to tempt her and worried that Annie might be coming home early, Aide dashed into the front room and peered through the net curtains. Was that Annie? No, just some random passer-by. When he returned from the other room, Lucy was closing the case.

'I'm glad there wasn't anything in there, Aide,' she said. 'Honest, I'm glad for you. I'd better go before she gets back. Wouldn't want her to get the wrong idea.'

The absence of evidence should've made things better. It should've helped repair the void between Aide and Annie, but it only seemed to be growing wider. He continued meeting up with Lucy at the pub.

'Absence of evidence isn't proof of innocence,' Lucy said, echoing Aide's thoughts. 'I'm sorry, I shouldn't say that.' She took a swig of her shandy. 'I expect my ex didn't always have hotel reservations and condoms in his briefcase.'

And so that growing thought returned. Perhaps they should check again. Where was the harm in it?

'It's not like there was anything marked "Top Secret" in there,' Lucy said.

'Yeah. Just a bunch of stuff.'

And so it happened again. Just like last time. And, no, they didn't make out. Aide wasn't the unfaithful one in his marriage. He wasn't doing overtime and going on work trips. And who was going on those work trips with her? Her boss? Who was he? Not that Aide knew that the boss was a 'he', but it was a natural assumption. Annie never mentioned her boss, but there must be one. If the boss was a woman, there'd be no need to hide it.

Once again he stood by Lucy's side while she twisted her picks in the lock until the catch snicked open. Once again, she sent him to check a noise, to check to make sure that Annie wasn't returning, but when Aide came back to give the all clear, he saw Lucy easing a scrap of paper out from the side of the case. Or was she easing it back in again?

'What's that?' he said.

She jumped.

'Oh, I'm sorry, Aide.' She held it out. 'It might not mean anything.'

He took the scrap and read a date, time and location. That was all that was written on it. A rendezvous? He began to rifle through the briefcase.

'Be careful not to upset the order or crease anything,' Lucy said, 'or she'll realise.'

Aide carefully followed her instructions on how to take things out and put them back in again so that the case wouldn't look like it had been tampered with. There was nothing else of interest.

'We'd better put that back as well,' Lucy said, indicating the scrap. 'I'll do it. I remember where I found it.'

Aide gave it to her and gloomily walked away, leaving her to tidy up and relock the briefcase.

A date, a time and a location. He had to know. He had to be sure. He didn't mention his plan to Lucy. It wasn't fair to involve her. Besides, he didn't want any misunderstandings. He wasn't going to be the guilty party in divorce proceedings. The contents of that scrap of paper stuck in his mind. He saw it in his dreams. He saw it whenever he looked at his wife. His wife keeping secrets from him. He had a right to know.

He wore his dark coat with the hood up and dark jeans. A casual walk down the street. He was just some passer-by. He glanced around at the buildings, searching for a number. What had he been expecting? A glitzy pad? A discreet apartment? A hotel? A dingy B&B? This wasn't a residential street. It was a business park. The location had just been a number and street name. Maybe it was in a different town?

Here was the number. Just a dull office block. Mostly dark, with a few outdoor lights. He looked around and spotted a couple of cars parked down the side, in the gloom. Was that Annie's car? No obvious sign of any nightwatchmen. He walked across the forecourt, around the side of the building. Yes, that was her car. So this was where she met him. This was their clandestine meeting place, where she was doing her so-called overtime. He must be the boss, and this must belong to the company, and he was using it for his little assignations.

'Step away from the vehicles and raise your hands where we can see them.'

Aide winced in the glare of the light beamed straight at him.

'I was just looking for my wife. That's her car.'

'Put your hands flat against the wall.'

'I was just–'

'Do it!'

What was the worst that could happen? Be charged with trespassing? But he wasn't breaking in. He had simply spotted his wife's car, and was coming over to investigate. Surely no one could make a case out of that. It would certainly be very bad publicity for the company, especially if it came out about the philandering boss. He glimpsed a figure in the gloom. Just some jumped-up security guard.

The realisation that the security guard wasn't alone hit him at about the same time as the wall smacked into his face, and deft fingers frisked him without any regard to his personal modesty. He would definitely be talking to his solicitor tomorrow.

'Step inside.'

He was hustled through a side entrance and into a room where he found Annie with a man.

'So,' Aide said, attempting a nonchalant pose, 'that's your boss, is he?'

'No,' Annie said. 'She's not here. He's from Special Branch. Why did you do it, Aide? I trusted you.'

'Do what? I happened to be passing and saw your car.' She wasn't going to make him the guilty party. 'And don't give me any of that trusted crap. You've never trusted me. You never tell me anything.'

'You've landed me in such deep shit. But they found your prints this time.'

'My prints? What are you talking about?'

'You've been photographing the documents in my briefcase and selling them to a hostile state.'

'What? No. It wasn't me. You're just a secretary. What would you have in your briefcase?'

'I handle our R and D documents.'

No, this couldn't be for real. But then he thought about Lucy — Lucy, who had never revealed her surname or occupation or address, who knew how to pick locks and rifle cases, who had sent him to act as lookout. Lucy, with her ridiculously old-fashioned long gloves that wouldn't leave fingerprints.

The man from Special Branch began to tell him about his right to remain silent.

SMALL TALK

Patrick Linehan

For weeks before the Conference both sides were engrossed in putting their arguments together. They war-gamed the opposition's expected reactions to all of their points. All knew that the meeting needed to be held though, in their mutual antipathy, nobody wanted it. The smoke of their midnight oil stung their eyes for sleep was a distant memory. But it would be worth all the effort they told themselves, for the Americans had a surplus of wheat and the Russians, who had a shortage, were in the market to buy.

Three days before the meeting, the senior American called a halt to any further work. His team had begun to go over old ground and, becoming testy with each other, had sunk to 'playing the man rather than the ball'. They were ordered to take time off; to go walking; to re-acquaint themselves with their half-forgotten wives and families; revisit their hobbies. In fact to do anything which was not work. He needed them rested and mentally alert.

By contrast, the Russian opposition struggled on, full of distrust and with various hierarchical levels constantly overruling the ranks inferior to them. Thus, only one person held any decisive sway and he was powerless without Moscow's clearance.

The morning of the meeting, a Monday, was taken up with meaningless pleasantries; tongue-in-cheek glorification of the achievements of the Socialist Soviet by the Americans, without referring to the near starvation of the Russian populace, and a harangue from the Russians on the evils of the capitalist lackeys of the West.

In the afternoon, someone on the American side, in frustration at the lack of progress, mentioned the subject of wheat. The Russian lead winced and, shortly thereafter he and his team got up and left, without explanation.

On Tuesday, the Russians were in their seats early. Yes, their smiling interpreter said, they could talk about wheat. What about wheat? the lead American asked gingerly, fearing repetition of the flat silence of the Monday. The interpreter looked at his lead and said that Russia would like to buy wheat. The Americans laughed aloud in relief at the admission, a number of the team all talking excitedly at once. The lead Russian screamed at them, barked at his own team and motioned them out of the room. An alert American interpreter buttonholed his opposite number asking him in fear, what had they done which was so out of place. The Russian said he didn't know.

'Will we see you tomorrow,' he asked.

'I don't know,' said the Russian.

After a gloomy evening, a sleepless night and without much hope, on Wednesday morning the Americans trudged, from many different directions in the interests of secrecy, to the meeting place. The Russians arrived late and sat down without apology. The lead American, deciding that he and his team could be better employed elsewhere, launched into a loud ultimatum that was meant to drown out any argument. His opposite number listened with a progressively pained expression and part way through the peroration, he shrieked at the American then led his team out as before. One of the Russians, dawdling, perhaps by design, said, 'Smalltalk. He need smalltalk.'

The American lead said, 'Goddamit. I smothered him with smalltalk, Monday.'

The Russian left.

On Thursday the Americans came armed with a cornucopia of saccharine expressions of interest in the lead Russian's family;

their lead, in reflecting rimless glasses, began brightly and loudly, 'I believe your wife is a commissar in the great Soviet army. You must be proud of such an achievement by the little lady. Our women're too soft, too yielding, for that.'

A cloud of fear swept across the Russian's face and he unfolded from his seat with the speed of a straightening jack-knife. Almost erect and, seemingly, about to shout across the table, the man fell sideways and onto his interpreter. Others in his team started back from his crumpled body, ashamed that the lackeys of the West should witness such Soviet weakness.

'Call a doctor from the Pentagon,' said the lead American. 'Quick!'

'An ambulance, sir?' someone asked.

'Gawd, no,' said the lead. 'Not yet. It'll get in the papers and Moscow reads our Press.'

When the doctor arrived, both parties had helped to lay the Russian out on the floor. On examination, his breathing was even and, with the exception of high blood pressure, his other vital signs were close to normal. While waiting for him to come round, the doctor carried out a cursory general check working from the top down. When his right ear was probed, the Russian — still out cold — recoiled from the otoscope and keened pitiably.

'Ear infection,' said the doctor. 'Wow, that must be real painful!'

'Smalltalk!' both interpreters whispered, as one, 'He meant 'quietly.'

FLAMES OF LOVE

Shirley Buxton

John dismounted and stared in disbelief. His bike clattered to the ground. There was his ordered, perfect world going up in flames. Smoke clouded his glasses, tears streamed down his face. Clara, his beautiful wife Clara, the love of his life, was being lowered from an upstairs window on a stretcher. A fireman was emerging from the smoking ruin, bearing the limp body of his darling daughter on his shoulder. His mind rushed him forward to be with them, to hold them, to help them, but something was wrong. His legs wouldn't move. His head wasn't working. Nothing in his body was connecting.

Consciousness returned but the nightmare continued. He had a blanket round his shoulders but he couldn't stop shaking. A neighbour was talking to him, uttering words that he couldn't, didn't want to hear. A member of the ambulance crew was bent over, holding his wrist. Shutting his eyes again, John tried to blank the picture of the blanket covering his wife's head and the word 'lifeless' from his image of his precious only child.

'Elaina is going to be all right,' another neighbour reported. 'But she's crying for her mother.'

John struggled to stand knowing he must go to his daughter, that she needed him, would be reliant on him. How would he cope? All he wanted was Clara his wife, who made his world worthwhile, Clara who gave him the reason to get up in the morning, Clara, who fitted his life with perfection. Fresh tears streamed from his eyes. How could he, John, face life? How could he look after their child born just three years ago, challenging and changing their former life? It was Clara who had shaped Elaina's upbringing, shielding him, so he could fulfil his dream as a newspaper correspondent. How could they cope without Clara?

It was now three months after that terrible tragic day. He had somehow survived the harrowing day of Clara's funeral. John still couldn't bear to think about the moment the hearse drew up in front of the house, the journey to the crematorium, the slow pace as they approached the chapel; and even less did he want to remember the service and the committal. And yet it was there, as clear as day, haunting him. He sought comfort in the flowers. Beautiful, fragrant blooms had covered that stark, hard coffin, disguising the harshness of death. He imagined Clara bursting out of that floral mountain, her youthful energy abounding as laughing she'd tell him it was all a mistake, everything was okay. He'd grab her round the waist and tell her he loved her and they would be together for ever. They'd hold onto each other until Elaina would run in demanding her place in the wondrous reunion.

Reality was demanding. The future was as difficult to contemplate as the recent past. He lived from day to day, doing what had to be done. Caring for Elaina gave his life meaning. He found a deep love for his child, much greater than he'd known before. The love she needed was the selfless, tireless, boundless love of her mother and he had to provide it for her. It was what Clara would have expected him to do. Somehow he had to transfer the amazing love he had for his wife to their child. At first John found it too difficult, he even found himself resenting Elaina being alive when Clara was dead. Talking with a friend John heard himself explaining that Clara would have hated for Elaina to have died in that fire. He was certain that it was Clara's self-sacrificing actions that had saved their daughter's life.

Clara's parents had wanted to take Elaina home and bring her up as they had their daughter before. It would seem to be the perfect solution. The old John would have only too willingly handed over all the problems he now faced, knowing that he could drop in anytime he wanted and showered his little daughter with gifts and treats. But the traumatic events had changed him. He now had to cope with a new self. He was driven by an unexpected force swelling up from within that demanded he bring up their child, just as Clara would have done. Turning down Tom and Brenda's offer was intuitive; though he assured them he would need their support.

John didn't think of it as a decision until much later. Should he give it more thought? Would it be fairer on the vulnerable three-year old to be brought up by her experienced grandparents? Could he really fill the role of mother as well as father? He would have to do just that. It wasn't the matter of duty; it was what Clara would expect of him. More importantly it was what he wanted and what he knew was right for Elaina. They were bonded together by love.

LANDINGS

Stuart McCarthy

The 'topping out' ceremony on new buildings happens when the final tile on the roof is placed and cemented. This marks the symbolic finishing of the building and the handover from the builders to the clients. It is accompanied by much celebration, champagne and handshakes.

For the people of the 'first colony' it meant an end to living in sealed units, the end to only going outside in pressure suits and the end of the separation of families. Once the 'topping out' was completed the dome would be pressurised and the families, waiting in planetary orbit, could come down to the surface and be reunited. Then they would begin their lives as 'first colonists'.

The planet, given the designation 'ES 25', as it was the twenty fifth planet to be discovered with 'earth similar' characteristics, was seven light-years away from Earth. People, both individuals and whole families had clamoured to be given places on the Colonial Explorer. There were so many that stringent aptitude tests were put in place, followed by searching interviews and medicals. The successful thousand were assigned places on 'Explorer' and sent on their journey to ES 25.

At the calculated time 'Explorer' (the 'colonial' part had been dropped after protests from historical societies who felt the word had unfortunate antecedents) dropped into orbit around ES 25 and the thousand (now twelve hundred; seven years is a long time in space) had their first glimpse of their new home.

It was essentially red, but with an orange tint in many places. A six-year-old boy, looking at it through a viewing port, smiled and said, 'It's made of saffron!' And from then on it was known as Saffronia.

The site chosen for the first landing, the first outpost of mankind on this distant world, was an enormous, lozenge shaped crater surrounded by huge mountains. Probes were sent to the surface to obtain accurate readings of the atmosphere and gravity. They reported back that the atmosphere, as expected, was far too thin to be breathable.

The plan was for the landing ship to detach itself from 'Explorer' and touch-down. The next part of the process was for the four remote storage and equipment modules to separate and land in a pre-arranged circular pattern. The ship itself would land at the centre of that circle. Then the radians, sixteen poles each some 250 metres in height, would deploy marking the circumference. One of the storage containers held rolls of thin transparent steel, known as transteel, and these were attached to the radians with hawsers fixed to the top of the pillar. Then, at the appropriate time, when all systems had been checked, the long process of hauling would begin. On completion, the dome could be sealed tight, then 'topped out' allowing pressurisation to begin. Successful pressurisation would mean that the families waiting in the mother ship could descend to begin their new life. That was the plan and it is a testament to human ingenuity that it worked, almost.

The landing was a spectacular show of pyrotechnics that would have been impressive if there was anyone there to impress. The containers fell, free from the central core, on schedule and most landed correctly. One crashed and split open outside the designated area. The only good thing about what could have been a disaster, was that it didn't carry anything vital to the safe functioning of the dome. It was emptied, righted and left where it was. Then someone thought 'outside the box' and suggested it could be integrated into the fabric of the dome as an airlock. to allow passage of bulky objects and large numbers of people.

The rest of the plan went smoothly and 'topping out' was completed with pressurisation scheduled for the next day. Technicians worked round the clock to integrate the new airlock into the dome. Pressurisation began, the seals held and many fingers were uncrossed.

Commander Mitchell stood in the centre of the dome, close to the airlock into the landing ship (well you couldn't be too careful, could you) and prepared to remove his helmet.

'Mitchell here. Preparing to open.'

'Roger that,' came the reply from Don Robbins, the man who would take over if this did not work. 'Rescue teams ready. Good luck.'

'Thanks Don, here we go.' He turned the seal, twisted it, held his breath, opened the faceplate and breathed. 'Mitchell here, air is good, smells a bit of machinery, pressure holding. Bring them down, Don, bring them down.'

SOME TIME LATER

'No, Tracy, no. I'm not letting you outside until I consider it safe to do so. And anyway, we only have limited supplies of oxygen, and they're only to be used for essential work. So no, you will stay in the dome for the foreseeable. Is that clear?'

Doctor Tracy Braidwood, botanist, and agriculturalist on Saffronia, looked at Commander Mitchell and played what she knew was her final card. 'Perfectly clear, but I would like you to consider the mission goals, particularly number twelve. The one where it says, "To explore and catalogue the flora and fauna of the planet."'

'Yes, yes, I know all that and my answer is still no.'

'Even if I go alone, and only take two oxygen tanks. I know the shuttle brought fifty fresh ones down from orbit fifteen hours ago. I just want to look; I won't do anything else.'

Mitchell's patience ran out then, 'Oh, for God's sake, go. Take your suit and your two bloody tanks, no more mind you, and just go. But you'd better find something pretty special to justify this stupidity.'

'I will try, and thank you,' she said.

The first thing she noticed was the space and the stillness. There was no wind and the thin atmosphere made the sky an almost indigo shade of blue. She walked carefully, low gravity made it easy, making a complete circuit of the dome to make sure her suit and tanks were functioning properly. Satisfied, she set off towards the foothills of the mountains that surrounded the crater. Fifteen minutes walking brought her to the start of the slopes, so she stopped and looked back.

The dome was sitting on the floor of the crater, surrounded by the deep orange rock with the lighter patches interspersed. It looked for all the world like an orange-pattern jigsaw. She herself, was standing amid one of these patches. It looked natural, she prodded it and realised she was looking at the first plant to be found by humans on Saffronia. She smiled and imagined the fame that would come; her name immortalised. *Saffronia Braidiosa*, that would be what she would call it. She checked herself, no time for self-aggrandisement, she had work to do. She picked a sample. It was light orange in colour with rubbery leaves that squashed into fibrous strands when rubbed between the fingers. She picked another frond and put the first flora sample taken on this alien world into a bag. She wasn't sure if it would be the 'pretty special' item Mitchell wanted, but she had to start somewhere. She looked up at the almost sheer ramparts of rock and decided to have a go at climbing, after all she was meant to be an explorer.

Mountain climbing in reduced gravity was easy, and she hardly broke sweat in getting to the top. There she stood, mesmerised by the panorama before her. The red colours of the planet blended into each other, mixed with dark blues and lilacs stretched out into the distance. A 'vision splendid', she thought to herself. Vibrant colours merging into darkness and the hint of everlasting stars.

Warning, oxygen level critical.

The message cut through her reverie, reminding her that she needed to get back to the dome. She changed the bottle and began her descent. It was then she discovered the universal truth that descending a steep slope is more perilous than ascending. What began as a quick, smooth movement quickly changed into a headlong flight and then to an out of control near fall. She stumbled, striking her arm on a piece of jagged rock. Warning suit depressurisation came the message. She could feel the air bleeding away. The suit began to contract and mould itself to her body. She tripped and fell down the rest of the slope. She could feel the impact as her faceplate hit and shattered. 'So, this is what it feels like to die' she thought as blackness enveloped her.

She woke with a blinding headache and the suit telling her depressurisation was complete and oxygen level was nil. If that was the case, she thought, then she was dead., but dead people don't have headaches and dead people aren't still breathing. She was lying face down in a patch of her orange-coloured plants. Surely not. She took another breath; yes, she was breathing something. She moved her head, crushing a small plant, and felt the passage of air. She took another breath. The idea that came to her was utterly crazy, but it had to be true. She sat up, picked another plant, crushed it, and breathed in its gas. Oxygen, breathable oxygen. Now to get home.

Walk, pick, crush, breathe, hold breath, walk, repeat. Over and over, over and over. That was how Tracy Braidwood made her way back to the dome. That was how the search party found her.

Walk, pick, crush, breathe, hold breath, walk. That was how she survived.

Much has been written of how this discovery opened up the exploration of the planet. Much more has been written of the development of the Braidwood mask that removed the need for bulky suits, But, for Tracy Braidwood herself, just being the first to see Saffronia beyond the crater walls was more than enough.

BRAN'S DREAMS

Stuart McCarthy

The planet that first became known as Saffronia had changed markedly in the half millennium since the first landing.

Then it was the spaceship commander Bill Mitchell who watched over the automated setting up of the first colony. He went alone to test out the atmosphere in the newly erected dome and uttered those great words that rival 'one small step' in the history books 'Okay Don, bring 'em down.'

It was not long afterwards that botanist Tracy Braidwood discovered *Saffronia Bradiosa*, or 'Air Plant' to give it the name by which it became known. Her discovery led to the provision of a planetary atmosphere and that meant that unhindered exploration of the planet was possible.

Now the colony had become Saffronia City and, although it occupied the same physical space it had grown exponentially and become increasingly more and more complex. So complex in fact that it could only be effectively managed by computers. The city had come to rely on its central computer for life support and the everyday running of the city. The central computer had become the brain of the city.

Saffronia City was laid out as a vast regular pentagon with towers at each point and a central tower that held the city systems and the central computer. The six towers, all built from a wide base, tapered to a needle-sharp point. Walk-ways, at vertiginous height, linked them and provided access to all areas. The central tower was massive. It was circular, having a base of a half mile radius and tapering to a point some five miles up. No one, or at least almost no one, had ever seen the top as it was almost always shrouded in cloud, as it was the day Bran was brought before the central computer to explain his dreams.

They had begun some years before. They were of strange places. Huge and fiery places, mountainous places. There was a vast flat plain; the gravity here was too great for anything over a centimetre in height to survive, yet even so there was life. The landscape was crisscrossed by moving lights.

Then there was a volcanic crater at the bottom of which was a single eye. Black, with fiery red veins standing proud, it was seeking, searching, looking for food, devouring anything that came within its vision.

These and more were Bran's night-time companions and although they didn't frighten him, they puzzled him.

They puzzled him enough to consult Boase, his tutor cum mentor. This had led to interviews with Saffronia's leading psychologists and psychiatrists which in turn led to him being referred to the central computer.

He made his way along the third level walkway, so-called because it was three miles above ground, to the central spire and waited by the doorway.

'State your name and business,' said a quiet voice at his ear. Bran started, whirled round, but there was no one there. 'State your name and business, then I can admit you.' repeated the voice.

'Who are you? Where are you?' Bran demanded, his voice held a tinge of fear.

'I am the central computer and I am all around you. Please state your name and business.'

'I am Bran Gregory and I have an appointment with the central computer.'

'Thank you,' said the voice, 'I will now open the door, once you are inside follow the yellow light. It will bring you safely to me.'

The door hissed open revealing a well-lit corridor. A single yellow light hovered near the ceiling, it began to move as soon as Bran entered. Bran followed. The light was obviously a higher-order computer than anything Bran had encountered as it kept station just a few feet away from him as he followed. When they reached a junction, the light would wait for him. Eventually, they arrived at a place that was obviously not designed for man. Enormous blocks of metal were dotted about the vast space. The light was harsh and the air crackled with static. No man could work in this environment, it was for machines only. The blocks were smooth with no hand holds, no walkways or ramps for humans to move over the surfaces. The great cubes stood in the middle or a vast ocean of space. Yet the machines were tended by industriously busy robots and other automated devices. They hovered and buzzed in any plane, needing no wires or pulleys to give them impetus.

Bran had heard of these gravity-defying machines but had never seen any nor did he believe the stories about them. Now he knew they were true. A machine came up and stopped in front of him. It was a small cylinder with a sphere at the end and it reminded Bran so much of a dog that he couldn't help reaching out to pet it. To his surprise the machine let him touch it. Previously, when he had tried to touch one of the city's maintenance robots it had either shied away or administered a severe electric shock but this one seemed to welcome the attention. Despite himself he laughed, 'Hello there,' he said.

'I see you have made the acquaintance of one of my dog-bots,' said a voice by his ear. Bran whirled round, but there was no one there. 'Have no fear Bran, just follow the dog-bot, it will take you to a room specially prepared for our meeting.'

The dog-bot moved away and Bran followed. Wherever they went a walkway would mysteriously appear, guiding Bran to his next destination. The robot floated beside him, gently nudging him in the way it wanted him to go.

A smaller cube appeared. It had a hole in the side and a walkway directed Bran towards it. Inside there was a low table, an armchair and a desk. On the desk was a file with his name on it. He flipped it open, and began to read what was there. It was basic information about him but there were also accounts of his dreams and in the margin of one of them was written the comment 'Similarities with Jarrett'.

'You know you shouldn't be reading that,' said the computer voice beside him.

'Then why did you put it there?'

The computer gave out a very strange noise, a noise Bran could only liken to a chuckle. Was the computer laughing he wondered?

'Good point,' said the voice, 'now, please, sit, and let us talk.'

The armchair was very comfortable and could almost have been made especially for him which Bran would not be surprised to know that it was. The central computer was all-powerful in Saffronia.

'You have been sent to see me because you have been having dreams. Is that correct?'

'Yes,' said Bran.

'Bran, let me tell you,' the computer went on, 'you are not alone. Others have had these dreams before.'

'Others?' said Bran.

'As far as I know there have been four others, and there will certainly have been more. The last one I know of is Brian Jarrett.'

'What happened to him?'

'I don't know but he was having the same dreams as you are. They troubled him deeply, but he regarded himself as a rational being so he ignored them. He did, however, decide to record them so as to investigate further. We found his notes when we searched for him after he disappeared, He described the images in great detail, so much detail in fact that I was able to identify one or two of them from our interplanetary probes.'

'You mean what I am seeing is real.'

'Most assuredly.'

'Where are they from? What do they mean?"

'I think they are leading you towards the centre of the galaxy. But where the journey ends I cannot tell.'

'You said there were more. What happened to them?'

'They disappeared.'

'Will I disappear too?'

'I don't know, but it seems likely. I have read Jarrett's notes and know that your dreams are following the same path. But he did have one final dream and it was that dream that gave him a name. It was the last thing he wrote. Braidwood.'

'Mount Braidwood?'

'I think so.'

Mount Braidwood, the highest point outside Saffronia City and revered as the mountain first climbed by botanist Tracy Braidwood on her epic voyage of discovery nearly five hundred years ago.

'So you think I'll be called to Mount Braidwood sometime soon.'

'Yes.'

'What do I do about it? What do you want me to do about it?'

'That is up to you. I can't, won't interfere in your free will. But, if you consent I will watch you. Now you can return to the city and wait for the dreams. There is no need for us to meet again but I will keep watching. Is that acceptable?'

Bran nodded.

'There is one more thing I would like you to do for me.'

Bran looked up, 'What?' he asked.

'Keep talking to me. Tell me everything that is going on with you, everything you are feeling. Tell me anything you can remember about the dreams and tell me what you intend to do.'

'You already know what I am going to do.'

'Yes, I do, and when you get to Mount Braidwood keep talking to me. Will you do that?'

'Yes,' said Bran.

Back in his home, Bran prepared a bag for a short journey and left it by his bedroom door, ready.

He did not have long to wait.

It was a landscape similar to Earth, or much like the images of Earth stored in the computer archives. The ocean stretched to the horizon, but on the horizon there were clouds of the most beautiful lilac. They swirled around the mountain peaks that Bran knew were of the deepest obsidian. Above the clouds the sky was a deep green, a green that was mirrored by the glassy surface of the totally still ocean.

Bran stood on the shoreline, watching. It seemed to him that that was what the dream wanted him to do. As he stood a ripple appeared on the surface to be suddenly replaced by a gigantic head.

The creature was reptilian, with huge jaws and bulging eyes. Its body was long and sinewy, and as more and more of it emerged it coiled around Bran's body trapping him. The head towered over him, its breath pure sulphur. It spoke one word. It was the word Bran had been waiting for and it meant that his dream quest was nearly over.

'Braidwood,' it said.

ß

The only breezes on Saffronia are to be found at the top of the many mountain peaks. So said the guidebook. It went on to say that here a gentle breeze cools the weary traveller who has made it to the top. Bran was not weary, he was apprehensive and excited all at the same time.

What would happen to him? Would anything happen? Would he survive, or be changed, or left the same? He did not know.

'Computer,' he said, keeping his promise, 'here at the top it is very quiet. There is the usual breeze blowing but nothing else is different. I hope this is getting to you and you are finding it useful, even though I have nothing to describe.

'Wait a minute, the breeze has dropped, now it is perfectly still, and there is a change in the light, it's getting darker. Does this mean they're coming for me? Is this what you have been waiting for?

'Now I can see a shaft of light moving towards me, it's narrow and searingly bright. It's coming closer, is this what took the others? Maybe I will see them.

'I don't think I have long left, the light has almost reached me.

'Now it's all around me. I feel wonderful, peaceful and content, nothing bad is going to happen to me. I've never known such tranquillity.

'It's all around me, my body is shining, dissolving. I can see right through my hand. This is it. Goodbye computer, I hope you are getting all this. Light, weightless, floating. I can see so many others.'

The central computer watched the beam of light touch the top of Mount Braidwood and knew that Bran was gone. He had joined the others for what purpose the computer did not know and that irked it. It was one of its programming features to inquire and to find out. Bran had added much to his investigation of the phenomena it called 'The light'.

'Farewell Bran,' it said to itself, 'and may good fortune go with you.'

What would happen to him? Would anything happen? Would he survive, or be changed, or left the same? He did not know.

'Computer,' he said, keeping his promise, 'here at the top it is very quiet. There is the usual breeze blowing but nothing else is different. I hope this is getting to you and you are finding it useful, even though I have nothing to describe.

'Wait a minute, the breeze has dropped, now it is perfectly still, and there is a change in the light, it's getting darker. Does this mean they're coming for me? Is this what you have been waiting for?

'Now I can see a shaft of light moving towards me, it's narrow and searingly bright. It's coming closer, is this what took the others? Maybe I will see them.

I don't think I have long left, the light has almost reached me.

Now it's all around me. I feel wonderful, peaceful and content, nothing bad is going to happen to me. I've never known such tranquillity.

It's all around me, my body is shining, dissolving. I can see right through my hand. This is it. Goodbye computer, I hope you are getting all this. Light, weightless, floating. I can see so many others.'

The central computer watched the beam of light touch the top of Mount Braidwood and knew that Bran was gone. He had joined the others for what purpose the computer did not know and that irked it. It was one of its programming features to inquire and to find out. Bran had added much to his investigation of the phenomena it called 'The light'.

'Farewell Bran,' it said to itself, 'and may good fortune go with you.'

CONNOR AND MEGAN: A TALE FROM THE PLAGUE

Alison Court

Connor and Megan met at university. They were friends for quite a little while, before they took the plunge and became a couple. They were happy, smiley people. Megan was pretty and clever, outgoing and fun, and she had the happiness conferred by self-confidence. Connor was a big, cheery, bumbling boy, loyal to his friends. Megan was his first girlfriend and he was even happier than ever.

Now they were starting out on their careers, both in London. They thought about buying a little flat together, but lo, the Plague came suddenly upon them and they were separated from each other at a stroke. Connor lived with his brother in a small flat in Kennington. Megan lived with her family somewhere in a field in Surrey.

For a few weeks they made do in the same way as everyone else in the world was making do. They called each other many times every day and kept laughing and smiling but Connor was starting to ache inside. He wanted to wrap his arms round his girl and hug and hold her. He wanted to be quiet with her as well as chatting and laughing. He wanted . . . well, he wanted normality. He was a normal boy.

Megan's birthday was approaching. For the last two years he had tested out his fledgling cooking skills. For Megan's Birthday Year One he had cooked pasta and stirred in a sauce from a jar,

121

which, in a way, he had done very well and Megan had laughed and looked at him lovingly, appreciative of the fact he had done it himself and done it for her. For Megan's Birthday Year Two he had progressed to *spaghetti alla carbonara* and no, he had not bought a jar of sauce, he had made it himself, having asked his mother for details of how to cook his girlfriend's favourite pasta dish.

Now he had to make a splash. Blow the Plague! He was going to do something that would make Megan's birthday, well, fun. And it had to be better than last year.

Thinking hat on. What to do? There came a brainwave — he was going to make some pasta — from scratch — and he was going to deliver it to her doorstep.

He started to investigate. There must be chemistry involved. How else could just two ingredients turn into a dish as ubiquitous as pasta? Flour and eggs — simple. Flour was difficult to come by in the days of the Plague, he'd seen that on the news, but he also knew there was an old-looking bag of flour at the back of a cupboard in his brother's kitchen, because he'd had a rummage for late-night feasting only . . . well, last night. Eggs? Well, if you looked for them in the corner shop every day, you'd be bound to find them sooner or later.

He was set. He cleared away the detritus from the kitchen work surface and, in a moment of sentiment, wiped it over with a damp cloth. With many a referral to the recipe he found on his phone for 'Real Pasta', over the next few hours he laboriously conjured up a dish of his very own homemade ravioli, filled with feta cheese and spinach. He suspected feta wasn't quite the thing for ravioli, but this was after all the time of the Plague and you had to make do. And besides, he thought of himself as a modern man in matters of spinach, ever since he had gone travelling on a shoestring with his friends and they had lived on bags of spinach and, when they were flush, tins of sardines.

Dish of ravioli prepared, cooked and placed in a carrier bag, his mission now was to deliver it to Megan. He'd been puzzling over

122

that the last few hours, as he rolled and cut the pasta. Megan lived many miles away, not even in London. He'd been there on the train before but of course that was out now, as were buses. "Eureka! I've got it," he triumphed, "a bike!"

Out on the street, sure enough, there was a stand of rental bikes that looked to be in reasonable working condition. He'd never thought of using one before; they were, in all honesty, a bit small for him, but they did have two wheels, which meant exercise — and liberty. He tapped in the code, released the bike, hung the bag with the pasta dish in it over the handlebars and set off south.

It was quite a journey. Thank goodness there was less traffic than at normal times but all the same, it could be a bit hairy when some macho driver — and Connor had thought he knew about macho drivers, being a little bit of one himself — swerved past him at top speed. He clattered ever southwards, passers by turning to look at this big cheery man on a bicycle that was too small for him, carrier bag swinging, fragrant smells wafting in the breeze, as he made his way even further south than rental bikes had ever been seen before.

At last, after more than two solid hours of cycling — except for when he had to stop to straighten out the pasta dish, which was in danger of turning upside down and disgorging its load into the bottom of the bag, and except for the occasions when he realised how madly he was pedalling in the wrong direction — he arrived at Megan's doorstep.

He leaned the bicycle against the hedge, took the dish out of the carrier bag, laid it on the doorstep, rang the bell; he stepped back, hastily running his hands through his dishevelled hair. After a minute or so, there was at last the sound of footsteps and yes, the voice of his lovely girlfriend, "It's all right, I'll get it."

The door opened, and there she was, after what felt like so long apart. Connor's smile wrapped right round the corners of his face and suddenly he was speechless. He flung his arms out and so did Megan, as they looked and gazed and laughed at and with each other. They each stepped forward a tiny step but it was early lockdown days and they knew they may not hug. But it was almost as if they were hugging. Megan peeked inside the dish and gasped — her favourite and made by funny old Connor. They laughed and talked and laughed.

"It was my worst birthday ever and now it's the best ever," Megan said, as they parted.

Connor got back on the bike, no longer laden with pasta, and cycled back northwards. He was tired now, not used to cycling so far and besides, the adrenalin of the occasion was wearing him out, but nonetheless, by the time he returned the bicycle to its cradle after some five hours, he felt it was the best five hours he had spent in a long while.

HOW IT REALLY WAS

Avril Suddaby

I guess you all have heard the story of Goldilocks and the Three Bears. In the original versions of the story Goldilocks is a rather dim little blue-eyed blonde who does not behave herself very well. Not only does she wander off and get lost in the woods (Very Stupid), but she also enters a home uninvited (Very Rude), steals food (A Crime) and has the nerve to go to sleep in someone else's bed without even asking.

Now I am going to tell you what really happened. On that day a meeting was to be held in the Three Bears cottage to discuss the serious problem of the Big Bad Wolf, who was pestering little girls walking in the woods and terrorising old ladies who lived alone. Recently his activities had become even more malevolent. He had destroyed two or three houses on the Pigg Estate and he had quite illegally decided that everyone crossing the bridge over the river to get to town, should pay him something which he called the Troll Tax. Something had to be done. So the Woodcutter called a meeting of all responsible citizens of the Fairytale Kingdom to discuss what to do. Of course Goldilocks was invited as she was indeed a sensible mature girl and not the vapid blonde of the usual fairytale.

She arrived early at the Bear Cottage. This was because she often helped Mrs Bear with her baby and also did various household tasks for her. When she arrived the Bears were out, probably, she thought because the parents wanted Baby to be tired so that he would sleep during the meeting. Goldilocks let herself in. To her surprise the kitchen was in a mess – most unusual for the houseproud Mrs Bear. A half empty porridge pan was on the table with dirty bowls, cups and spoons. Goldilocks washed up and tidied everything away and then looked around to see what else she could do before the Bears returned. She went upstairs to see if the beds needed making.

When she went upstairs the mystery of the messy kitchen was solved. Although the Wolf was lolling on the bed wearing the mobcap which Granny Bear used when she came to stay, Goldilocks wasn't deceived for one moment. She screamed which woke the Big Bad Wolf. She realised she was in great danger alone in the house with him and there might be quite some time before rescue came. She thought quickly about what to do. The Wolf leered at her and said, "Come here, my dear, come and sit beside me on this nice comfortable bed."

Quick-witted, she embarked on the rigmarole of, "Oh my, what big eyes you have, Granny!"

And so on. All playing for time in the hope of rescue. But as we know, after "What big teeth you have, Granny!" the end is nigh. And still no sign of the Bears nor of the arrival of those who should come to the meeting.

So at this point clever little Goldilocks said, "Do you know about the meeting this morning? Everyone will be coming. And look! Look out of the window, Granny. Here's the Woodcutter with his Axe coming down the path."

Goldilock's ruse was successful, because from where he was lying in bed, the Wolf couldn't see out of the window. He was very afraid of the Woodcutter and his Axe, having had some narrow escapes in the past, so he jumped out of bed, ran downstairs and fled.

And that is how it really was.

THE LETTER

Moira Newlan

It had arrived on a Tuesday: a brown A5 envelope with '*City Council*' stamped on the back. She had assumed it was another bill. There were plenty of those. Rent, rates, gas, electricity, water, internet provider, suppliers, deliveries, marketing material.

At first, all those financial obligations associated with opening a small business had been overwhelming, but three years later, Shona now took it in her stride. She was organised, every file clearly labelled and regularly updated, every receipt handed over to her accountant. He, in turn, documented each item into Income and Expenditure spreadsheets, knew exactly what grants and allowances to claim, deducted his own modest fee and saved Shona a sizable sum. Indeed, her profit margin was higher than she had ever imagined and, in recent months had risen exponentially, as had her reputation.

The accountant, as with all her other staff, liked working with Shona. She kept her equanimity most of the time, even in the most challenging situations. Only occasionally she lapsed into a torrent of foul-mouthed expletives to the great amusement of anyone listening, while profusely apologising when the moment had passed. Whether it was her humanity or the undoubted provocation of the circumstances for such an outburst, Shona was easy to forgive.

She had leased the building in a residential part of town. A few decades ago, it would have a been a large corner shop, supplying its neighbourhood with everything from bottles of milk to the daily loaf, cans of spam, exotic tins of peaches, bars of green Fairy soap and the local gossip.

Now, the airy café buzzed with happy chatter, the clinking of china cups and saucers, and Shona greeting all her customers by their first names. Customer service was excellent, as were the coffee and cakes.

With a limited budget, Shona had sourced all the crockery from charity shops. These were often sold in sets, with matching teapots, delicate milk jugs and sugar bowls. No-one wanted good quality china anymore — it was cumbersome to store, harder to wash and didn't fit the current mug and dishwasher lifestyle. She had commissioned her old Art College friends to re-imagine the premises and to source every item with a tight fiscal hand. A remarkable number of assorted usable tables and chairs had been found in skips or fire sales or second-hand office supply shops With a good scrub down, and extensive painting, the interior too had been transformed. In time, Shona thought, local schools might supply some artwork to hang on the walls.

From the outset, Shona had wanted to employ 'vulnerable' people. They would need to do most of the washing up by hand, as well as other chores. But surprisingly, the initiative had proved so popular that she had amassed a large waiting list of individuals both wanting to work and happy to work for nothing. A local charity heard about the café, and organised a rota where volunteers would work three days a week for a month. The charity had been quite astonished that so many had requested to stay on after their placement. But it was easy to see why. Volunteers had found a camaraderie and fellowship that many had never before experienced. Her staff now included a mixture of 'vulnerable' adults, job seekers, cancer survivors, and lonely pensioners. A couple of young lads had completed their week's secondment from the local College and shyly asked Shona if there would be any more work. She assured them that if any one left, or called in sick on a Saturday, they would have first option. She would let the staff manager, 'Marvellous Mary', have their contact details. She oversaw all the rotas, and was the first person to approach with any questions or concerns. She had been a godsend and taken a huge load off Shona's mind. Mary was just the sort of person she needed: organised, methodical, straightforward, motherly.

Shona had an idea. A couple of weeks later she approached the lads. She knew that they were musical. Would they like to organise a 'gig' on a Friday evening, from 5.30 till 7.30pm? She couldn't offer to pay the artists, but it would be an opportunity to perform in public and if, at the end of the evening, anyone wanted to donate, they were welcome to keep the proceeds as their fee. She would apply for a licence, and supply pizzas. Carlo, her irreplaceable Italian barista, would know where to find an authentic supplier. Friday evenings soon became a great success, with fledgling musicians eager to book a coveted spot. The demand proved so strong that ticketing had had to be introduced to control the numbers. Profits grew further, more than enough to cover any extra overheads.

It had been a challenging three years. The hours were long, with Shona's day beginning at 5.30 to bake the scones and cakes. In time, Shona asked other small entrepreneurs to bake cakes and cookies to supplement her own. It soon became evident that talent and skills could be found in abundance. Search around, ask the right questions and take a small risk.

After three years, Shona had built up a commercially successful business. It nurtured local talent, provided purpose to its staff members and had become a community hub. Customers enjoyed the friendly atmosphere; women of a certain age enjoyed their cappuccinos as well as flirting with the good-looking Carlo. The food was fresh and modestly priced. Smaller half portions were available for those with less of an appetite, or on a budget or a diet. In this respect, it bucked the trend, and won many-hearts.

When, on that Tuesday afternoon, Shona finally sat down and opened the brown envelope, she could not believe what she was reading. The Council was giving her notice to leave. The lease would not be renewed when it terminated in twelve months' time. A planning application had been made to demolish the cafe, make full use of the adjacent vacant piece of land, and turn the site into a block of flats. It would be no higher than the three-story terraced houses in the area, and with the pressure to provide much needed housing, it was likely to be approved by the planning department.

How was it possible, that in one moment, a thriving business, a vital community amenity, a venue for new talent, a respite for needy individuals, could be dealt such a cruel blow? How could her business be threatened by the solely commercial interests of an external agency whose only consideration was profit, who had smart lawyers and well-paid advocates?

But there it was, in black and white. A new battle had begun. There was no guarantee that she would win.

SMILE FOR THE CAMERA

Nicola L C Talbot

(Reprint of an ebook short story published by Dickimaw Books.)

Evelyn watched the array of rectangles arranged on the screen in front of her. The desk was covered in detritus: crumbs, fluff, stray hairs, and the desiccated corpses of insects. The computer hummed as its fan expelled hot air from the processors into the poky room, turning dusty cobwebs into miniature windsocks. The overhead fluorescent tube flickered, and the swivel chair creaked at her every little fidget.

Each rectangle on the screen showed footage from a security camera installed in a self-service checkout. Six rectangles for six tills. How many hours of her life had she spent staring at this screen? Alert for any customer who tried to slip by an unscanned item or where the barcode scanned didn't match the product in the customer's hand.

Old customers, young customers, confused customers, irate customers. Turning the products this way and that before the series of thick and thin parallel lines could finally be detected by the beady red light. The harassed employee — under instructions to direct all but cash-only customers to the self-service tills — appeared first in one and then another rectangle to deal with items that wouldn't scan or to inspect sturdy reusable bags that were heavier than the machine's maximum tare weight. At least Eve was able to sit back, with her feet up on the desk, munching crisps. There were definitely perks to this job.

An elderly customer came over to a till and slowly scanned her items, pausing after each product to double-check the screen. Finally, her age-worn face lined with worry scrutinized the screen one last time before she reached out a wrinkled arthritic finger to touch the payment option — not that there was much option for a card-only till. She glanced over one shoulder and then the other, her movements slow and stiff, before unzipping a handbag that hung satchel-style across her body. She bent her head, revealing a thinning parting in wiry grey hair.

Another zip inside her bag also needed to be undone before she eased out a black rectangular card holder. Eve recognised it as one of the RFID-blocking type. The customer glanced over her shoulder again before removing a credit card. Eve reached for the mouse and enlarged the window. A cautious, paranoid customer, but more concerned with shoulder surfers and skimmers than the camera which was aimed at her.

The customer's card had the type of design where all the information is on one side to make it easier to be scanned by mobile devices, because no one likes to tap in sixteen digits on tiny keyboards. Eve paused the video feed and zoomed in. The customer had oriented the card so that the blank side faced any potential eagle eye behind her, but this meant that the details were caught on camera as she moved it over to the payment terminal. Credit card number, name (Mrs A Smith), expiry date, card security code and signature, *Alice Smith*, were all visible in the still image on the screen.

Eve had two mobile phones: a regular one with a contract for normal use and a cheap device with a pay as you go SIM. She wiped the crisp grease from her fingers onto her jeans, took a photo of the screen with her burner phone, and saved it as a secure note.

Paranoid people were often too paranoid to have banking apps on their phones, so they didn't get instant notifications of purchases, and it took longer for them to discover fraudulent activity. They relied on multi-factor authentication, but credit card companies didn't always demand a verification code for every transaction.

Time for a little pampering. Eve checked that the VPN was connected and directed her browser to her favourite store. She soon had around nine hundred pounds worth of goods in the online basket. May as well round it up to a grand. She added a few more items, negotiated the checkout, and reached the payment page, where she entered Alice Smith's card details and waited while the spinning circle on the screen twirled. No request for a verification code. The transaction had gone through successfully.

Now the race was on to get as many transactions through as possible until the card was blocked. She went to another site, loaded up the basket, and tried again. This time there was a prompt to send a code via SMS for verification. Oh well, at least she'd got lucky once. She abandoned the order, closed the browser, and went back to work, alert for shoplifters and any more payment cards that passed across the camera or the movement of fingers over the payment keypad. Beep, beep, beep. Unexpected item in the bagging area. Assistance is on its way.

Eve popped a dark milk chocolate button into her mouth as she studied the pair of brown eyes that momentarily stared directly at the camera. This customer always used her phone to make the payments and she unlocked it with her fingerprint. Payment successful. Thank you for shopping at our store. Eve's tongue played with the melting blob of chocolate as she watched the customer walk away, a shopping bag in one hand. The glass doors slid open in front of her and, just in the corner of the rectangle that was showing the video feed, Eve saw a car door open. As the vehicle reversed out of the parking bay, the registration plate briefly passed through the frame. Eve made a note of the number before selecting another chocolate button. This one she nibbled on, until she had to lick the remnants off her sticky fingers.

She ought to be content with the easy pickings, the low-hanging fruit, but that was like expecting a shark hunter to net goldfish. Eve swivelled her chair from side to side as she contemplated the brown eyes and the locked phone with its digital wallet. She replayed the video feed, watching the customer put down the basket on one side and her bag on the other. Tap on the screen to start, and then out with the phone to scan her loyalty card. The card was accepted. The membership number was visible on the screen. Eve looked it up in the store's database and found a mobile phone number associated with the account of Roberta Mallory.

It was inevitable in such a small town that Eve should one day spot a registration number she recognised amongst the row of parked cars as she walked up the high street on her day off. Pretending to window shop, she scanned the shoppers and pedestrians for the owner of the brown eyes and the digital wallet and the nice car. She ambled up the pavement, weaving around buggies and nattering mothers and a huddle of teenagers. Eventually she found her prey sitting alone at a table in a coffee shop, caressing her phone's face with her thumb.

A bell tinkled as Eve opened the shop door, and she nonchalantly walked across the laminate floor to the counter. The barista, whose name tag identified her as Carol, put down her cloth and greeted Eve with a smile.

'What can I get for you, my lovely?'

The barista's ears were pierced along their curved edge, with small gold studs like notches in a tally stick. Her uniform was covered in stylised coffee cup icons with steam curling into a cursive C. Three friends at a corner table gathered their coats and bags, laughing and chattering and promising a return fixture the same time next week. The bell over the door jingled, telegraphing their departure.

An overhead fan wafted the scent of hot milk, chocolate, herbal teas, and coffee beans. Eve took her time examining the board listing the available beverages, before pronouncing her choice: a cappuccino, please. She lounged at one end of the counter, whilst

Carol the barista prepared her order, and accessed the 'forgot my password' page of a common messaging app. She copied Roberta Mallory's mobile phone number from her secure notes and pasted it into the form, but she held off tapping the submit button until she was in position.

She switched over to the camera app, started a video recording, and held her phone up in the coffee-infused air, stepping from one side to the other, as though searching for a better signal. A machine gurgled behind her. She lowered the phone and checked the video feed. It showed the shoulder and side of the face of her prey and, just beyond that, the screen of the coveted device.

Eve switched back to the form and tapped submit. A verification code has been sent to your device. Back to the camera app, and another wave in the air with the frustrated look of a person vainly searching for reception.

'Chocolate or cinnamon on top, my lovely?'

'Chocolate please.'

She lowered her phone and played back the video. A buzz raced through her as she saw the notification pop up on her prey's screen and there, for a brief moment, was the verification code. She quickly typed it into the text box and turned a beaming smile on the barista. She paid for the coffee with cash, tossed the change into the tip jar, and went over to a table.

For a while, she contented herself with just inhaling the thick scent of hot, freshly ground coffee emanating from her cup while she took over her victim's account. She would drink it later. Time was of the essence in this game. It seemed that Roberta was variously known as 'Bobbie', 'Bob', 'Bertie' and, although it was possibly a typo, 'Bee'.

Eve scrolled through the list of message threads and found one simply labelled 'Mum'. Her fingers tapped over the virtual keyboard. Mum, I need your help. I'm in such a mess. The response was swift. Oh no! (Open mouth emoji.) What's happened? (Face screaming in fear — Roberta's mother was clearly an emoji aficionado.) Back and forth the messages went, an often-used story of woe and an urgent need of funds. The responses were peppered with an assortment of pictographic reactions. Of course I'll send you the money, love. How much? (Two hugging face emojis and a winking face throwing a kiss.) Eve sent her bank details and then, with a flush of anticipation, switched over to her banking app, waiting for the promised increase to her balance.

The bell tinkled as another customer came into the shop, temporarily letting in the street sounds until the door closed. Carol the barista went to work on a latte. Nice weather we've been having lately. Oh yes, that's such a change from last week. Haven't seen you for a while. How've you been getting along? Well, you know how it is. Oh, I know. Will you be going to the street parade next month? I hear they're cutting down the number of floats. Seems like everything is being cut back except the cost of living.

'Mum' was taking her time. Perhaps she had poor digital skills. What if she was asking someone for help? Someone who might advise her to first check that the message was genuine. Perhaps she might call her daughter, who was still sitting at the other end of the café, tapping at her phone. Eve sipped her coffee. She ought to get out of here. Her victim might guess it was done by someone nearby. But she wouldn't be able to prove anything. You can't just leap up and start flinging accusations at a stranger who's minding their own business. No, she would brazen it out. There was no fun in life without a bit of risk. The tingle of adrenaline was like the sparkle in champagne.

The screen on the banking app went blank as the page refreshed. The little circular throbber spun round, its rays pulsating as it turned while the device fetched new information. Heedless now of the coffee, her attention was solely focused on the phone. The load icon disappeared, and new text appeared on the page, but instead of the promised funds, the account was frozen. A chair scraped against the hard floor in front of her. Eve looked up to see a familiar pair of brown eyes studying her, but instead of the indignant rage of a victim there was an amused smile. The supposed victim sat down opposite Eve.

'Of course I'll send you the money, love,' Roberta Mallory said. 'Hug, hug.' She held her hands up against her face, mimicking a hugging face emoji, 'Kiss, kiss.' She pursed her lips and winked.

'I don't know what you're talking about,' Eve said. 'What's this all about?'

'It's about my sock puppet account you took over, and my little sock puppet mummy you found. You're nicked.' She leant over and plucked the phone from Eve's limp hand. 'Let's see what else we can find in here, shall we?'

STIMULATED BY A CRUISE
Patrick Linehan

Jim and his wife, Patience, had had a routine existence. The irreversible, joyous sounding, snap of the marriage-lock; an unremarkable bungalow; the usual nine-to five. For him, labour in the overworked garden crammed with vegetables. For her, the thrifty housekeeping and part-time working. And, shared between them, the upbringing of four children.

Now, in the afternoon of their lives, they worked with their customary stoicism, paying off the mortgage, the largest of their prudent, adjudged as manageable, loans. Loans which had been taken out to fund the passing years during which their outings and holidays were to be managed so as to be affordable, restfully pleasant, and restorative.

Jim and Patience made a team which played the game of life astutely, but within the limitations of the hand it dealt them.

Unlike Patience's uncle Marion. *Uncle*? Yes. For his mother had wanted a girl; she got, instead, a wire-haired, uncontrollable cyclone of a child who developed, through his teens, into a merchant sailor. In short order, Marion rose through the rollicking ranks to captain his own ship. Life was good, he had a girl in most ports and fathered bastard children in both civilised and uncouth territories. He was successful in everything he did and was soon the owner, not just of his own ship, but a shipping line which, in time, was shared and managed by his offspring. He, himself, wouldn't live ashore, where he could have had his choice of playboy villas, and the attentions of statuesque, air-headed, and pneumatic women, but preferred to live afloat on the most luxurious of his ships.

But, regardless of his aversion to a stable lifestyle, Marion would, sometimes, visit — unannounced — the staid bungalow of his niece and, regardless, perhaps, because of their silent, purse-faced, disapproval, he would torture her and Jim with lurid accounts of seafaring nefariousness and landfall release from pent-up cabin fever. He always brought his own bottles when he visited and would swig, with a broad grin, from one of them while tempting a recoiling Patience to join him. He would recount the fights that had left their marks on his leathery features, or pull aside the curtain of his shirt to bare purple, jagged scars as evidence of near-miss stabbing attempts. Before leaving them, he would sing, loudly and on their very doorstep, ribald versions of sea shanties such as 'South Australia' or 'The Shoals of Herring.' Afterwards, the neighbours would smile wryly, accepting his behaviour as familiar. Jim would 'tut'; and Patience would protest that there was 'no real harm in him'.

Until, that is, one day at the hairdresser's, all other material having caught the attention of the clientele, she was left with no other choice of reading matter than one of the more scurrilous, red-top, newspapers. On page 4, and just after the main daily salacious pictures on page three, there loomed a large photo of her 'harmless' Uncle Marion. The picture looked downwards at a review of his latest ghost-written book giving a full and frank, no holds barred account of his many and varied exploits (and sex-ploits!) both on land and sea. Jim and Patience were referenced under the thinly-veiled and contrived aliases of 'Fred and Freda', a stolid couple portrayed as unadventurous and devoid of ambition or aspiration. The cheek of it, she thought, and closed the paper as noiselessly as she could muster in case any rustling would generate an erroneous insight into her literary tastes to the other waiting customers. There and then, Patience resolved to put Uncle Marion out of her mind and to break with her tolerance of him, and his shenanigans. On his next visit, she planned to give him a focused mouthful of criticism which he could not misinterpret.

Months passed, and then, one day while watching the one o'clock news, Jim and Patience were shocked to see pictures of a blazing ship, prow pointing at the sun, sinking in the sea-lanes off the coast of Syria. It appeared that an Allied submarine had launched a Cruise missile 'by mistake'; the consensus was that the stricken ship was a victim of 'friendly fire'. Allegations, it was reported, also abounded that the ship was carrying a contraband arsenal to rebel forces operating across North Africa, an arsenal that must have been seeded with tell-tale tracking devices which would have made the ship a certain target.

'Sounds like something Marion would get up to,' said Jim.

'He wouldn't sink that far,' said Patience, hopefully, and, looking this time, to him for confirmation, said: 'There's no *real* harm in him. Is there?'

'He didn't get where he is today without sailing close to the wind,' responded Jim, and, as an afterthought, said: 'In a manner of speaking, that is.'

The possibility that it might have been something Marion might have got up to arose, again, three months later when the morning's post brought a letter that landed, weightily and with apparent portent, on the mat in the hallway of the 'staid' bungalow. A cursory examination of the contents revealed a maze of 'heretofores', 'herinafter's, and 'whereas's' scattered among other clusters of equally baffling mutations of language. What the letter seemed to intend, was to inform Patience that her Uncle Marion had been 'killed, at sea, in an unfortunate accident'. Further, that the considerable royalties from his books would devolve to her and would 'henceforth' be payable to her; there was only one proviso and that was that she must read all of those books and widely publicise their merit and availability. A happy outcome,-and one which stimulated by a 'Cruise', would

141

bring her to examine, and extol, the writings of her departed uncle more closely.

Patience was surprised at the ease with which she created a public persona for herself, and took to calling herself 'Trixie' when she gave readings, She affected a tinkling laugh, and would become wistful when presenting 'Fred and Freda' as 'Uncle's little joke', a grown up version of how he would tenderly tousle her hair when she was a child. He had never done such a thing, of course; for that matter, who even knew that he had a side-line in writing books? But he had bequeathed to her an unexpected frisson of pleasure by putting her so far out of her comfort zone.

Today, Patience can afford to embrace the creed that one can never be too thin or too rich; she can often be observed in various discreet lounges across world, sipping, here a Singapore Sling or there a Horse's Neck while offering surreptitious, flirty-though-mature encouragement to young men, of the rugged entrepreneurial type, to improve themselves through reading Uncle Marion's books. After the initial jolt which he felt at such departure from her norms, Jim continues to hope that there is unlikely to be any real harm in that, though he does reflect with some resigned foreboding, that she is the niece of someone who — to use the red-top vernacular — 'did put it about a bit'.

THE NIGHT OWL

Shirley Buxton

I need my sleep, but occasionally I am a night owl.

My night time regime starts with a visit to the garden. Armed with a torch, a pot and a small persuading stick, I embark on a slug hunt. Slugs or snails invading my vegetables are gently transferred into my collecting pot which is white so I can easily see if my little friends are trying to escape. The slimy creatures are then transferred to their new home in the brown garden waste bin. There they have food in abundance. I can't bring myself to kill them even in a beer-filled bath.

It is so peaceful outside when most people are getting ready for bed. It's a time when the sounds of nature take over from the racket we humans make throughout the day. If the hedgehog is about, then the slugs have a different fate, being tipped out into her pathway as she rustles her way round the back of the children's play house and behind the compost bins.

Pausing to breathe in the cool night air, I take in sounds of owls. Not just owls hooting, but owls screeching and barking, a sound distinctive from the call of a fox. Looking up into the summer night sky, I watch the midnight blue in the northwest change to black. I hope to catch a glimpse of an owl, but they are too busy hunting. For the past month, the delicate scent of a flame orange azalea has drawn me to another part of the garden, but now this is fading and the heavy perfumes of honeysuckle, rose and jasmine fight for my attention. I close my eyes and absorb the heavenly smells and sounds.

What I love best about this solitary time in the garden is the Moon. Her mood changes nightly. Sometimes she is slow to wake or doesn't appear at all. There are nights when she hides coyly behind the clouds, peeping out tantalizingly before disappearing under billowy covers. Each night I watch her progress as she waxes and wanes. I yearn to reach up and caress her crescent curve. Beneath her watchful gaze, my night time garden glows and its mood changes too. My attention is suddenly caught by the song of a blackbird with insomnia. Is that going to be my fate tonight or will I go in to bed and sleep?

When Moon reaches her fullness, night takes on a special brightness that can't be rivalled by any sunlit day. Those are the nights when I don't sleep. My mind is alert, not wanting to miss the many splendours of the night. Looking through dormer windows, I follow Moon's path, enjoying her splendour. This is our time, just Moon and me. Star patterns lose their sharpness to her beauty. Will she draw me back outside away from my bed? I smile as I unlock the backdoor remembering the childhood rhyme:

'Girls and boys come out to play,
The moon is bright as light as day.
Leave your supper and leave your sleep,
Join your play-fellows in the street.'

My slippered feet take me back into the garden. I toast Moon with hot chocolate. She is not wearied by her long westward journey. As we smile at each other I am aware of birds stirring. A quarter turn clockwise from where 'yesterday' disappeared just a few hours ago, a pale light dances on the horizon. Silhouettes of bats returning to their roosts pass across the grey-blue light of dawn. It's first light, so I bid good-night to Moon before going indoors to bed. The excitement of the night is over. Now I can relax and sleep, serenaded by the dawn chorus.

HE PULLED THE TRIGGER

Stuart McCarthy

Billy O' Reardon died of patriotism. That wasn't what physically killed him, old age did that. It was his soul, that died that day. Some say he was a patriot, others that he was a traitor, but then one man's freedom-fighter is another man's terrorist. You pays your money and you takes your choice.

Billy O' Reardon was fourteen when I met him. He had just heard de Valera speak at Skibbereen. de Velera had spoken for a long while and said many things but his theme 'Ireland for the Irish', planted a seed in Billy's heart. On his way home he passed a churchyard. A large part of this cemetery was given over to a mass grave. Here hundreds of Irishmen, women and children, victims of the Famine, were interred.

Their bodies rolled into a huge trench and quickly covered to prevent disease spreading. The very inhumanity and injustice of it fired the teenager's inbuilt anger and he vowed, there and then, to join the Republican movement and push the hated English out of Ireland.

His home wasn't far away, but he did not go there. The happy go lucky teenager that was Billy O' Reardon never went home. What returned to the loving parents was a committed Republican volunteer. Oh, he assured them he was all right and had just been visiting friends. That was the first of many lies he was to tell them. His new friends were like-minded men who welcomed into their midst, an idealistic teenager.

'Where's my rifle?' Billy asked after he had sworn allegiance.

'Ah now, don't you go getting yourself all fussed about that. You have to earn one', I told him.

'And how do I do that', he responded.

'When your moment comes, you'll know.'

Then I sent him home to await instructions.

They came a week later. A week in which Billy jumped at the slightest sound and became increasingly withdrawn and alone.

Then, on the Sunday, after Mass, a man he did not know came up to him and spoke the code word.

'Be at the crossroads at ten o'clock,' he was told.

'What'll I tell my parents?'

'Ah now, you'll have to think of something, won't you?' then the man left.

Billy went to his room around nine and slipped out of the window. He was concealed by the crossroads at the appointed time. I was driving the car, and at first failed to spot him, so well was he hidden. But as I slowed, he emerged from his hidingplace, his frail figure picked out in the headlights.

He climbed into the back alongside two other volunteers.

'Where are we going?' he asked. 'What are we going to do!'

These and other, similar questions were greeted with silence. It's never a good idea to discuss a mission with anyone, least of all with an unproven boy.

The mission was a police station in Owenahinche. It was easy, we got in, took the files we wanted and left. Back in the car we noticed Billy had a rifle, almost as big as himself, and several bandoliers of ammunition.

'Now what have you got there?' I asked him.

'A rifle, to kill Englishmen and traitors.'

It was the look in his eyes, the dead, flat expression of hatred, that made me wonder just what we had done to this boy.

I made sure he wouldn't be anywhere near the shooting end of any future operation we mounted and it frustrated him. Even though he was employed only as a messenger, lookout and general runner he always took his rifle with him. It was a part of who he was, of what he had become.

It was about this time that Michael Collins returned to Clonakilty. He had been born there, and he sought to use that fact to try and get us Republicans to agree to the Irish Free State. Although not perfect, Collins argued, it was the best we would get if we didn't want years of civil war. We, for our part, didn't want an Ireland shorn of the six northern counties and weren't prepared to go along with his proposals. But we decided to listen to him anyway.

'Send a messenger,' my commander said, 'tell him we will meet him in Clonakilty market place.'

The messenger was Billy but I made him leave his rifle behind before he left.

'Why?' he asked.

'Because you're going to see Michael Collins.'

'Then I'll kill the fecking traitor.'

'That's why you're leaving your rifle here, And the pistol you have in your pocket, leave that too.'

Billy gave me a look that would have curdled milk but reached into his pocket and drew out a Webley service revolver. It looked huge in his hand and I doubted if he could hold it steady enough to shoot anything but I took it from him anyway.

He came back four hours later.

'What did he say?' I asked.

'He said he would meet with us.'

'Where?'

'Where we said?'

'And when we said?'

'Yes.'

'Grand, now go home and don't come back until I send for you.'

'Why? I want to be in on it.'

'I'm sure you do, but no, not this time. Leave this to us.'

'You're going to kill him?' the voice hopeful, eager.

'No, were going to listen to him.'

Billy reacted with fury. 'You're going to talk to traitors. That makes you traitors as well.' He stormed out of the house. That was the last I saw of him before the day.

We were waiting at the appointed place for Collins to arrive when a friend of Billy's approached.

'Billy's got some friends to mount an ambush to stop Collins coming,' he told us.

It was then we heard gunfire.

We got there as quickly as we could. As we turned the corner, into a small valley we saw the situation was stalemate. The firing was all coming from one side of the valley. The Free state soldiers were sheltering behind their armoured cars. Neither side could move without being shot.

It was when I looked to the other side of the valley that I saw Billy and he was looking at just one target, Collins.

I saw Collins standing, striding behind his troops, directing their fire.

I saw Billy settle over his rifle.

I saw him take aim.

I saw him pull the trigger.

Three died that day. The man that was Michael Collins, the soul of Billy O' Reardon and the hopes of a peaceful Ireland for a generation.

THE MILLER'S DAUGHTER

Alison Court

Once upon a time there lived by a stream that ran through the fields a Miller and his beautiful daughter. In fact, he had three daughters, but the older two had left home to live in the town. The oldest had married a rapacious innkeeper and worked endless hours in his tavern, and the middle sister worked in a miserable cellar somewhere, so all that was a bit disappointing.

Anyway, there came a morning when the Miller found his youngest daughter sitting on the banks of the stream, weeping her eyes out. "What's up with you, then?" he asked, in as tender a manner as was his wont.

"I'm just so lonely, living out here in the country with you, dear Father," she replied, "and dear as you are," for he was only quite dear, not wholly so, "I can't help but feel there must be more to life than being a Miller's daughter."

"Well, valuable as you are to me, dear Daughter," said the Miller, "it is obviously time we put it about that you are in need of a suitor."

"Oh, but Father," wept the daughter, "is that the only answer you can come up with? I can't help but feel there must be more to life than just being subservient to the needs of one demanding man or another."

"But, Daughter, we are in a fairy tale, and yes, that is the only way." And he set about letting the world know — or at least that small part of it where anyone might be interested — that he had a beautiful daughter who was ready for marriage.

The local gossip network did its job well, and in no time there were three suitors lined up to be interviewed by the Miller. Rather surprisingly, the first was a prince, but it turned out it wasn't that surprising, as a) he was really not at all good-looking, b) he was really not very nice, and c) he was jolly old. The second was a handsome soldier, and he looked like he might not be a bad bet, but his minus points were also threefold; first, he was penniless, second, he was away fighting most of the time, and thirdly, he was rather macho and only thought women were good for one thing. The third suitor was most unlikely. He was a frog, and his minus points were therefore very obvious and too many to count.

Nevertheless, the Miller, having interviewed all three suitors, thought he ought to go through the traditional triple test period, as that, after all, was supposed to come up with the ultimate perfect solution to any conundrum and often unearthed the most surprising positives to a character.

He summoned the three suitors to his mill.

"The first test I want you to undergo," he said, "is to obtain for my daughter a basket of rosy apples."

Now, that, dear reader, sounds very easy, but since this part of the story took place in springtime, this test was not all it first appeared. The prince set off on his white horse and snarled to himself, "Pathetic little test, I'll get some from the castle shed. They'll be all right." And off he went. Meanwhile, the soldier barged off into the nearby village, thrust his sword at a village woman and made her give him the last of her remaining apples from the previous season. And the frog hopped off, and we don't know how he got them, but he managed to get hold of a basket of apples.

All three of them returned to the miller. The prince whipped away some damask from the basket containing his apples, and lo, they were Golden Delicious, so that was no good. The soldier opened his sack and poured out a meagre pile of worm eaten and rotting apples that might have been rosy once but now they were definitely past their best, so that was no good either. And the frog heaved and hauled behind him an enormous handmade basket of woven willow and in it, beneath a crisp linen cloth, there was a bountiful array of the most beautiful rosy blooming apples that had ever been seen in olden days.

One up to the frog, then, and the Miller's daughter looked pale and anxious.

The Miller called the suitors to order and announced the second test. "I want you to prepare a perfect home that will be fit for my beautiful daughter," he said, and looked confidently at the prince, thinking that this must be where he would score a bit better.

The prince went off and thought, "I don't have to do much here, I've already got a perfectly decent castle. That's bound to win." The soldier went off a little thoughtfully. He'd never set much store by having a home, he'd just got away with sleeping in hedgerows or ditches or on the bench at the tavern. Still, he'd come up with something. The frog hopped off, and again, we don't know how he did it, but he got together a home to offer the Miller's daughter.

All three of them returned to the Miller and suggested to him that they do a little tour of their various proposed homes and off they all set. First of all, they went to the prince's castle, but quite frankly it was rather large and grey and it wasn't in the nicest part of the kingdom, surrounded as it was by very unhappy-looking peasants and poor hovels. It rather gave the impression that he lorded it over poor people and didn't do anything to make their lives better. So that was rather disappointing. Next, they went to the soldier's brilliant offering of a home and that turned out to be a bivouac. Fair enough, he'd furnished it with a straw mattress on the ground, but it wasn't really the sort of prospect to turn a Miller's daughter's head. And then the frog took them to see the really very beautiful home he had built, on the banks of the stream, only further towards the town, and it was full of love and decent furniture and it was just the right size, not too big or grand but not too small and poky.

Two up to the frog. The Miller's daughter looked even more pale and anxious, though she had to admit this frog had something about him.

The Miller called the suitors back in front of him and announced the third test. "I want you to tell my beautiful daughter, here and now, a story with a happy ending," he said, as he looked again at the prince who must surely be a literate sort of fellow, having had all that education at expensive schools and posh universities.

The prince stepped forward and started to tell a story all about how privileged he was and what a very special place that gave in the world to anyone lucky enough to win him, and the icing on the cake was that his castle contained absolutely everything any wife could want and she needn't ever step into the outside world again.

The soldier told a story of derring-do, that involved a lot of swashbuckling and galloping about on cliffs and thundering along on sandy beaches, and the especially happy end to the story was that he always won every battle and so his services were required for evermore by great leaders wanting to make war.

The frog pulled himself to his greatest height of about eight inches, expanded his chest with air to speak, and spoke. He felt quietly confident. "Once upon a time," he started, "there was a handsome young man. He lived in a comfortable home, nothing flashy, and he had proud parents, so they encouraged him to be a student. He worked hard and read all the books he could. He wanted to make his way in the world. But his tutor knew his young student might eclipse him in the academic world. The day came when the young student wrote a perfect piece of work and instead of rewarding him with top marks, as one might expect, his tutor instead cast a spell on him, turning him into a frog, to punish him for being cleverer than he should be. The tutor wasn't completely wicked, however. He included a let-out clause, which was that if any beautiful young Miller's daughter ever kissed him on the cheek, he would turn back into a handsome and clever student again. Then he would take her to live happily ever after in a beautiful house in a beautiful place, and they would live in mutual respect and harmony for ever more."

The frog cast his eyes down. He didn't dare look at the Miller's daughter. But, "Oh!" gasped the beautiful Miller's daughter, "That is a terrible but a wonderful story, and how amazing that it is so pertinent to us." And she cast her arms around the frog and kissed him on the cheek.

Straight away there was a flash of lightning and a lot of stars, and the frog no longer stood there. Instead, there was such a handsome young man, with lovely brown eyes and a big flop of hair over his brow, and a lovely smile and rather nicely dressed to boot.

"May I marry you?" he asked shyly. "I love you very much and I think I have proved myself with the three tests, even though these gentlemen," and he indicated the prince and the soldier, "love you as well, and have worked hard to fulfil the requirements laid down by your father. By the way I am not madly into dictating to any woman what she must and mustn't do. I would like to live together with you for ever in perfect harmony and mutual respect, and I hope that's okay with you, unusual as it is in this day and age."

The Miller looked utterly confused and wobbled about a bit. But the Miller's Daughter clasped her hands and said, "Oh YES, that would be wonderful."

And they truly did live happily ever after.

MARIANNE NORTH: ARTIST — 1830-1890

Avril Suddaby

I like to think of my heroine Marianne, when she was a young girl, reading a book about China with a puzzled frown on her face. She is reading about how the feet of Chinese girls used to be bound so that they would remain small. Tiny feet, like lotus flowers, were much prized. But the price Chinese women paid was high, they were crippled and could only totter along taking the smallest steps. Marianne is appalled, she wonders whether there are any parallels between the treatment of girls and women in China and those in Europe. Marianne herself recently suffered the indignity of her first corset to control her developing body. She is not happy about the 'honour' which this garment, obligatory for a young lady, has bestowed upon her. Even worse, she imagines, might be future restrictions forced on her by the values and mores of Victorian society. Where and when, she wonders, will the boundary be when she will refuse to conform.

After the usual basic education given to girls, Marianne occupied herself with music and singing, dancing and horse riding, and sketching – all her the usual pastimes for a young lady of the time. Every summer, after Parliamentary sessions were over, Marianne travelled in Europe with her sister and father, who was MP for Hastings, and whom she adored. When Marianne's mother was dying, she had made Marianne promise to look after her father, a promise which Marianne had no problem keeping. After he lost his Parliamentary seat, the two of them spent most of their time travelling; and her artistic talents developed. At first she did landscapes in watercolour, and then moved on to botanical art and painting in oils. Soon painting flora became a passion for her.

When her father died, Marianne lost not only her chaperone but also her best friend and companion. Although she was by then a 39-year-old spinster, she soon decided she wanted to travel again. In part to help her overcome her grief at her loss. She set off to Italy with her servant Elizabeth as a companion. However, Elizabeth hated travel, was often in tears, wishing she, "had never comed", and it was a relief for both women when Elizabeth was put on a steamer at Genoa and sent back home.

Thereafter, Marianne travelled solo. Over the next 16 years, she went twice around the world with only brief spells at home in England. Among the countries she visited were Canada and the USA, Jamaica, Brazil, Tenerife, Japan, Singapore, Borneo, Java, Ceylon, India, Australia, New Zealand, South Africa, the Seychelles, and Chile. And all the time she painted obsessively, producing hundreds of pictures. Over 800 of which still survive, mostly botanical art but sometimes landscapes.

These bald factual statements do little to reveal her remarkable story. This was in the days when the conveniences of modern travel such as planes and international hotels, now taken for granted, did not exist. Marianne used whatever mode of transport she could find, and if and if nothing else was available she hired mules. And if that was not possible, she would hire a local guide and walk. She stayed in whatever sort of lodging house was available, or if there was nothing she would camp. Because she was in search of rare, exotic and beautiful plants, Marianne didn't keep to the well beaten trails. She braved isolated, dangerous places, jungles and risky climates and places where infectious diseases were prevalent. All this in order to find the most perfect specimen for her painting. She was sustained by her passion for her art. Such a life was unusual and courageous for a middle-aged Victorian spinster travelling alone.

I have beside me a photograph of Marianne sitting at her easel. She looks very like Queen Victoria. She is wearing a long black dress, and her hair is gathered in a bun at the nape of her neck. It is impossible to know if she is wearing a corset, but I suspect and sincerely hope not.

I imagine Marianne trekking through a hot, humid jungle, following a local guide who has promised to take her to a waterfall where some rare orchids grow. She has heard about these orchids and is determined to include them in her collection. But here in the jungle there are no flowers to be seen, because all growth struggles up to the light above the thick forest canopy. There is only dense green foliage, and any flowering plants here are either climbers or parasitic bromeliads, all too high for her to see.

Marianne is hot, sweaty and dirty in her long black dress. Itchy from numerous mosquito bites; she plods uncomplaining, along the rough uneven track behind the guide. He has taken other Europeans into the jungle, usually to track down exotic animals and sometimes to trap or shoot them. He is amazed at this new client, a middle-aged spinster, who has shown more resilience and stamina than the men who had previously hired him. Last night she slept in a primitive tent which he had made to give her some shelter. In the evening they'll return to camp to spend another night under canvas.

"Not much further, Missie," he says to encourage her. Marianne nods.

Soon they hear the sound of the waterfall, the trees thin out and some light penetrates the gloom of the jungle. A minute more and they emerge into bright sunlight. The sun makes sparkling diamonds in the cascade and there is a rainbow in the mist above the water.

The guide tells Marianne that this is the place, and if they climb up the rocks at the side of the waterfall, she will find the prized orchids. He helps her climb, handicapped as she is by her long dress. Soon he spots one specimen, then more, delicate perfect little flowers glowing with vibrant colours. When he points to the flowers, Marianne is overjoyed. She chooses which flower to paint and he helps her set up her easel and stool, then leaves her so that he can rest and smoke nearby while she works.

When the light starts to fade, they return to camp, where the boy, his assistant is guarding the mules. He will have a meal ready for them. The following morning they will ride back to the village. The guide's one remaining task for his remarkable client is to organise her transport back to the city. Then he'll be paid handsomely for his work. For the next few months his family will have no money worries.

Inevitably this lifestyle took its toll on Marianne's health. Suffering from the after effects of rheumatic fever and increasing deafness, she had to stop travelling in 1883. Her last trip was to the Seychelles. Although she found a previously undiscovered rare orchid, the trip ended unhappily. The islands were subjected to quarantine because of smallpox, and the drunken brawls at Christmas and New Year frightened and shocked her. Travel was becoming a self-inflicted duty and she found herself surprisingly glad to return to England.

Back home, in retirement, the inexhaustible Marianne embarked on two final projects: the writing of her recollections, and the construction (at her own expense) of a gallery in Kew Gardens to house her paintings. Joseph Hooker, who was the director of the Gardens, accepted her offer with alacrity. She had by then become well known in botanical circles and had had four plants named after her.

Marianne's paintings, mostly quite small works in oil, are unique. Largely self-taught, her work does not belong to any recognised style or genre. Botanical illustrations are not usually set against a background of their native habitat, as Marianne's are. The use of colour brings to mind the Pre-Raphaelites, and the pictures are like jewels, mini-visions of paradise, usually depicting exotic flora although sometimes small animals, birds or insects are included. Among the botanical paintings, which fill almost every inch of the walls in the Marianne North Gallery, there are also a few of her beautiful landscape paintings showing the places she visited.

Her autobiography, entitled *Recollections of a Happy Life,* acknowledges the hospitality and help given to her by friends, acquaintances and the many strangers who she met on her travels. There is little mention of the hardship and danger which she endured. Rather than write about her privations, her book is full of enthusiasm for the natural beauty of the countries she visited and her passion for the flora which she hunted down and then captured in their native settings.

Marianne North was a remarkable woman, who did not allow herself to be restricted by convention and developed her talents to the full. If you don't already know the Marianne North Gallery, I urge you to visit when you are next at Kew Gardens. It is completely unlike any other gallery you will ever visit, as idiosyncratic as its creator.

THE MOVE

Moira Newlan

They had moved back to the city centre, having left it twenty years earlier for a leafier, larger life in the outlying suburbs. Now they wanted a more manageable home, with less of everything; less garden, fewer rooms, less worry, less expense,-and more time for themselves.

Ages and stages, they both agreed, had driven the move, fuelled by last winter's heavy storm damage and the unpalatable prospect of a new roof.

They had spent months in preparation; clearing the loft, the garage, the garden sheds. *Good to have a purge.* The mouldy child's car seat, rusted garden tools, broken shelves and electrical items, redundant computer desk, imperfect suitcases, all disposed of in various visits to the city's dump. The large mower, electric hedge clipper, two old bicycles — sold on eBay. Old toys and books and paraphernalia — transported to numerous local charity shops to spread the donations and profit.

As the moving date grew closer, the difficulties in downsizing a family house, full of such evocative and resonant memories and sentiments, grew greater. Which books to take or leave? Which raincoats, overcoats, winter, summer shoes and clothes? What vestiges of a child's life to keep? For the medals, scrapbooks, school reports, cards, and drawings, meant more to them than to the children. Which papers, files, sundries, plugs, and keys were useful still? Those cycle-bags, roof-rack, spare this and that, only needed occasionally, but would they ever be needed again?

Meanwhile, they existed in that chain of mutually-dependent buying and selling properties in an uncontrollable web, liable at any time to a threat, a withdrawal, an inexplicable delay, or solicitors 'on holiday' and unreachable. Anxiety rose with the blood pressure.

By the time they moved, both were thoroughly exhausted in mind and body, alleviated with unrivalled relief. Drained by the effort of decision making, and by the unpredictable logistics of the property industry.

Nagging doubts pressed into their brains, though neither wished to confide their misgivings.

Had they chosen too quickly? Should they have sold and rented, waited for their perfect new home? They knew the city well, the range of options, knew what they did *not* want. But the synchronicity of properties for sale at the time of searching, proffering a perfect solution, seldom, if ever, exists. *Get 80 percent right, and you'll be doing very well* advised an estate agent friend of theirs. They compromised, to please each other, to fit sufficient, though not all, criteria, and avoided a daunting interlude of renting.

Within a few months, they had settled into their inner- city apartment. They had almost cleared their temporary storage unit, reluctantly accepting that those items would never find a place in their new home. They enjoyed the views, the shiny kitchen, the fashionable new bathrooms, and numerous socket points. Walking to the city centre was quick and easy. Transplanted shrubs and bushes on the large balcony offered a token of their old garden.

Sarah thought about her delicate heirlooms, the old leather sofa, the leaded glass desk lamp, given away in the effort to divest and unburden, and secretly wanted them back.

Gordon missed the back of the garden where he used to make a fire, smell the newly cut grass or stare at the stars.

Sarah missed the fruit trees which would be blossoming by now, her capacious upstairs wooden cupboard, her walk in pantry, the decoratively coved ceilings she had painted herself.

Gordon struggled to find space for his tools and special pieces of wood. He wondered if he would ever make anything again.

Sarah missed the birds and the hedgehogs who visited unannounced, the peace and tranquillity.

Gordon missed his large capacious study with all his books and maps and treasured objects, and his old wooden armchair where he used to sit and daydream.

But neither shared their thoughts. In time, they would adjust and accept. They could always move again.

ART AWRY

Patrick Linehan

Edouard was angry. His *amour* had spurned his advances; what had made her outright rejection of him even more unbearable was that she was abetted in it by her mother — a woman who, in Edouard's youthful, creative mind had all the qualities to make her detestable. He thought her blowsy; incipiently jowly; narrow at the shoulder; broad at the hip. Moreover, she would tolerate no meeting for the lips of her daughter and Edouard's. She poisoned the mind of her daughter against him and, deliberately and with malice aforethought, she put about unsupported rumours of perversion and loucheness among those with whom he associated. Some of those rumours had sprung from a seed of truth of course, which only meant that they sang more sourly in the ear of his *amour*.

Ahh! How Edouard yearned for his Yvette Poupette, as he fondly called her. And oh! How coldly she eyed him, disdain and antipathy sitting haughtily on her downy features.

'Why, why, why?' he was wont to ask her. 'Did she feel like this about all young men?'

No, she said. Just him.

'But why?' he plaintively asked again.

'Because,' she said, a faraway vision of unspeakably heinous things scudding across her trembling visage.

'And my mother —' she said, as if referencing the Oracle at Delphi.

And so Edouard immersed himself in his work, painting canvas after canvas while mentally whirling, dancing or howling before each one in keeping with whichever dervish of the day possessed him. Strangely, the quality of his output was superb. Every piece sold for a purseful of dry and dusty gold which he threw, wearily, into the misshapen drawer of his bedside cupboard careless that, in transit, it might fall into the gaping jaws of his chamber-pot.

One canvas, however, resisted all his efforts at selling it. He hung it high; he hung it low; he stood it on gallery floors and yet despondently carried it home at the end of day. It was a well-wrought woodland scene, he thought; in the forefront sat two men, one bearded, seemingly expounding on some weighty subject; the other looked out at the artist, surprised at being caught in the glare of the paint brush. Further into the scene, a dark-haired woman in a diaphanous wrap stooped decorously to dry her feet. Edouard titled it 'Le Bain'. Critics were harsh with it, though, deeming the three characters disconnected, ignoring each other, and thus giving a cold and slapdash impression of separateness and a lack of any cohesion as a group. Insults poured down on him like hail, but Edouard affected disinterest.

All this, and much else of his existence as an artist, was irksome to Edouard. And then, he hit on an idea: Why not, he thought, combine his two life-irritants — the pictured scene and the mother of his *amour*; it would be a simple thing to put another figure into the painting, wouldn't it?

Acting on the principle that any hated and overweening characters could be encompassed by imagining them nude, he loaded his brush with a leftover sickly ecru paint and shaped up to slap it on the canvas to the left of the surprised — now with reason — man. An imagined touch on his arm, however, counselled caution; taking a few deep breaths, in the interests of commerce, he lovingly began to paint a shapely sitting nude. The only concession he made to his anger was to ensure that her very recognisable face looked out to the viewer. He threw a sheet loosely over the finished work, so as to allow the paint to dry,

168

wiped his hands on an oily rag and set off for the cafe to share a bottle with his friends, Emile and Berthe, and to eat.

A year later, Eduard's friends came to his studio on the way to deliver their submissions to the annual exhibition. Without revealing his painting to them, he knotted the covering sheet around the picture and, slinging it over his shoulder, they walked together to the *Salon des Refusés*, a well-known gallery where the best of second-class paintings were exhibited. Their prestigious exhibition would begin the following day and, although their commercial manager saw the piece as mildly salacious, he went on to say that even bad publicity would work in their favour; on those terms, he seemed to intimate, they were prepared to risk exhibiting it. Edouard said, with some truculence: 'I paint what I see, not what you want to see,' and left.

A week later, Eduoard's friends came to his door, excitedly describing a picture titled '*le Déjeuner sur l'Erbe*' which they had seen at the *Refusés* exhibition. Emile swore that he had seen the piece before and quizzed Edouard on the whereabouts of his '*le Bain*', which he was sure, had been plagiarised to form the basis of the object which saw queues of Parisians paying extortionate money to view it. Expectation was that it would be housed in the Louvre when the exhibition had finished. Berthe said to Edouard that he must see it for it had an uncanny likeness to his '*Bain*'; maybe the sequence of titling by the gallery had slipped a notch when the catalogue was in preparation.

The next morning, Edouard wangled admittance to the *Refuses* by a side door. He positioned himself so he could scan the audience; surely, he thought, Yvette would attend such a popular event. But no, instead, as his gaze swept the outer edges of the crowd, he gloated at seeing Yvette's mother craning to get a glimpse of the figures in the painting. Then, as she moved closer, he saw her pull her veil over her face; ignoring the buffeting from those around her, she stood before her image, as if transfixed. In the end, she tore her herself away and Edouard could almost feel a wistfulness in her as she faced him straight on. Then, seeing him,

169

she hurried across to him, her arms outstretched, her tiny fists bunched. He could only guess at the expression on her veiled face. She enveloped him in a bear-hug, her breath burning at his neck, her sharp little teeth agitating at his jugular.

'Edouard,' she said. 'Why didn't you speak up?'

'And s-s-ay what?' he stuttered.

She threw back her veil and consumed him in a kiss. She stood back, admiration — adoration — passion in her eyes.

'Why did you never say it was me you wanted all the time,' she whispered.

DECEPTION

Shirley Buxton

'Bye Queenie. I'll see you next Wednesday.' James closed the back door noisily before doubling back into the staff toilet. A few minutes later, hearing Queenie lock the shop door, he emerged. This was his favourite time of day, when the charity shop quietened to become his secret home. Earlier that afternoon a smartly dressed lady of a similar height and build to himself had handed Queenie two large John Lewis carrier-bags. Sneaking a quick glance, James had been sure there would be some great finds. The art was to take his pickings before the sorting gang took stock of what had been donated. Upstairs, James revelled in the soft textures and subtle colours of the materials. From that day's donations he selected half a dozen garments that he hoped would make a valuable contribution to his wardrobe.

Continuing his evening routine, James opened the trapdoor. He pulled down the ladder, before ascended into his garret bedroom. It had taken weeks of ingenious planning to acquire keys, a ladder and all that gave him a comfortable, secure place to live. Eagerly casting aside his day clothes, James slid into a stylish, cocktail dress. Even without the correct underwear, make-up and wig, he felt and looked good. This would be perfect for his date on Friday.

Life at his parents' house in Oxford had become unbearable. His sexuality was a burden that James felt he could not share. For years he had practised deception both at home and school. His parents, who had high expectations of him, thought he was studying Law in London. Each term they delivered their son to the

171

station. Three hours later he would be boarding the train from Liverpool Street to Norwich. Fortunately for James, student contact these days was mainly through mobile phone and e-mails. Creating fictional excuses for not spending long vacations with his family in Oxford, appealed to James' dramatic streak.

The introduction to this charity shop had been through Liz, a long-time friend of his mother, who volunteered in the shop on Thursdays. Three years ago, James' family had been to stay in her rambling house on the outskirts of Norwich. As a result of a staffing crisis at the shop, James was enlisted to help for an afternoon. A poor lad sheltering in a nearby doorway had set him thinking. What a paradoxical situation, charity shops empty at night while there were hundreds of homeless people. It had led James to embark on his present plan. The theatrical challenge of carrying off this latest daring deceit raised him to new levels of excitement. A major risk was that Liz would recognize him. Fortunately, boys change rapidly in teenage years. A drastic change of hair style and accomplished acting skills meant that he'd never had to use his well-rehearsed cover story. Having taken up residence, his original plan had been to invite homeless people to join him, but James was happy with his solitary life and was loathe the risk of spoiling what he had created, or to share his secret life.

On Wednesdays, he became 'Josh', casually clad in clean T-shirt and jeans, and turned up mid-morning to help Queenie for the rest of the day. Queenie had a soft spot for Josh. She liked his friendly helpful manner. He brightened her humdrum life that revolved around caring for a partially disabled husband. She enjoyed sharing her lunch with this boy whose mother never thought of sending him with food. Josh seemed particularly fond of her homemade quiche and sausage rolls. He was so thoughtful, always checking the back of the premises and obligingly leaving by the rear entrance.

Visit the shop on Mondays and you'd encounter shy 'Sylvie', assisting Madge and Rita. On Tuesday, student 'Mark' would appear about lunchtime, a little weary after a night serving behind the bar at the Theatre Royal, which supplemented the allowance from his parents. Clare and Grace were glad to leave the till to the quick-witted Mark while they busied themselves stocking shelves and rearranging the rails. Customers commented on how lovely it was to find a charity shop that attracted so many young assistants! Mark also helped on Saturday, their busiest day. The Friday team would be helped by 'Rob' or 'Janie', working on alternate weeks. The other staff enjoyed Janie's outgoing, bubbly nature, while Rob was renowned for being a 'bit of a lad.'

The greatest challenge was Thursdays when 'Emma' joined Liz and Rita.

'You know Liz, there's something about Emma that reminds me of Sylvie who helps on Mondays,' Rita had commented within James' hearing.

'I don't know about that, but for some reason she reminds me of my friend in Oxford. It could be her daughter except she only has a son.'

Emma carefully dropped into the conversation that Sylvie was a cousin, but their families didn't see much of each other, hoping this would distract Liz from her wonderings.

James enjoyed the challenge of sustaining his chosen characters and nurturing their unique personalities, but he loved the evenings. They belonged to him. In particular, he delighted in his expanding wardrobe. Tonight his hand swept across the rail to the evening wear. Discarding his day clothes, James savoured the sensuous silk caressing his smooth boyish skin. The intense peacock blue suited him. His slight build and gentle facial features did not require much make-up to complete his transformation. Pleased with his choice of accessories, James stepped out. Tonight was a new adventure. Liz had issued invitations to her fiftieth birthday party.

173

'I'm just having a few local friends over to celebrate. Emma, why don't you come? I could pick you up when I collect my husband from the station. You'd be a bit early but I'd love some extra help.' Emma had accepted.

'Be there about six-thirty. I'll be driving my red Citroen,' Liz had informed her.

When the red Citroen drew up at the station, it was not Liz driving.

'Are you Emma?' inquired the silvery voice that James had known since his birth.

THE ARRIVAL OF MAYBANK

Stuart McCarthy

We were clearing out mum's bedroom when we found it; a small, grey, teddy bear about as big as my hand with a white muzzle and a pink nose. I had never seen it before and was about the throw it away when curiosity, always the antidote to boredom, made me put it to one side.

'Mum,' I asked when I went downstairs, 'I found this in your bedroom. Where did it come from?'

Her eyes lit up and she smiled. 'Maybank;' she said, 'I always wondered where he got to. You've never met Maybank have you?'

'No, I haven't, is this him?'

'Oh yes, he was my most treasured possession for many years. He was a constant reminder of the goodness of people.'

I was interested, 'Tell me more,' I said.

'Well,' she said, 'it all happened so long ago and normally I wouldn't be able to remember much but with Maybank, I can, oh yes I certainly can.'

She paused to collect her thoughts. 'It was the May Day Bank Holiday and Stephen and I; Stephen was my young man at that time, went to the seaside to walk along the beach. I had been seeing him for many months and I thought he was going to be 'the one'. He seemed constant and very attentive and I had thought that this would be the time when he would propose. I had expected it to be so romantic. Us walking along the beach, hand in hand, then, at the appropriate moment he would turn to me, drop onto one knee and ask for my hand.'

She paused to smile to herself, lost in her own thoughts and I knew that she was there, on that beach, with Stephen. I had never heard of this Stephen so I assumed he had left the picture. Mum carried on.

'Well, there we were, hand in hand, when he turns to me and says, "Miriam, I am in love with someone else. I can't see you anymore," and walks off.'

'The swine,' I said, 'the absolute swine. What did you do? Did you run after him? Did you ever see him again?'

Mum just smiled and patted my hand, 'No and no,' she said. 'No, I didn't run after him, I was too shocked and no, I never saw him again. Perhaps for the better I think.'

'You would have killed him,' I said.

'Oh no, well brought up girls didn't do that sort of thing. No, I just stood there for a while, hoping he might come back perhaps. I don't know. Then I turned and made my way back into the town.'

'Where did you go?'

'Do you know, from that day to this, I couldn't tell you. All I know is that I ended up outside a small café in an arcade. It was one of those establishments that was screened off from the rest by curtaining and sold cream teas and morning coffees. Well, I must have stood there for a long while before the proprietress came out to see what I wanted. It was then that I started crying uncontrollably.'

'What did she do?'

'She took me to one of the tables, sat me down and gave me a big hug, 'It's a man isn't it?' she asked and I just nodded my head. Then she got up, went over to the curtains and pulled them across.

There were people outside but she pulled the curtain right in their faces and came back and asked me to tell her everything.'

'And did you?'

'Yes, right from the beginning, it just came pouring out. She listened and got up to make a cup of tea for us both. It was then she found Maybank. He was sitting on one of the tables that were not covered by the curtain. It had obviously been left there because there was a note with it. It read, and I can still remember those words, *'To the lady who is upset. I hope you feel better soon. An anonymous friend.'*

I picked up the teddy bear, it had obviously been well handled and clearly loved, Its fur was threadbare in patches where it had been cuddled over the years.

'And you never found out who it came from?'

'No, although I did put an ad in the local paper to try and trace this kind person but it never came to anything.'

'And you called it Maybank because . . . ?'

'Of the May Bank Holiday, when I got it.'

'Of course.'

'And then?'

'I took it home and it helped me through those dark days. Many was the night I cried myself to sleep with Maybank. I found I could tell him everything and he wouldn't judge, he would just listen. He helped me through the loss of Stephen before Dad came on the scene. Maybank was there at our wedding and was the first thing I packed when we went on holiday. He's been a great friend to me.'

'I wonder who the *anonymous friend* was.'

'That we shall never know,' said mum, 'but that simple act of kindness helped me more that he or she will ever realise. I was upset when I lost him but now that he has been found he can come with me to Sandy Cove. And when I die, I want you to have him as a reminder that not all people are bad.'

And that is exactly what happened. Mum spent the rest of her days in Sandy Cove Retirement home. Maybank had pride of place on her chest of drawers and when she died Maybank came to me. He sits on my bedside table and is a great listener.

CHALK CLIFFS ON RÜGEN

Alison Court

It's a beautiful May morning. The sun is rising, over the sparkling sea of turquoise and blue. Up on the slopes ahead, a gentle breeze touches the beech trees, that are just now bursting into leaf. The first outcrops of the high jagged cliffs of chalk are bathed in morning light. Everything is soft, golden. It is the perfect day for a scramble and a bridal couple, in the little port of Saßnitz, are excitedly tying their bootlaces before they straighten up, and head out from the pension where they are staying.

Caspar and his newly-wedded wife Caroline are, exploring the area around Greifswald, on the Baltic coast, where Caspar was born. Hand in hand they set off, laughing with happiness on this beautiful day. Even the sore in her heart for Caroline's long-lost brother, is deeply hidden; he hasn't been heard of since he left for Denmark fifteen years ago. No one knows what has become of him. For now, though, everything is a wonder.

Caspar hardly knows which way to look, whether at the clever and beautiful woman at his side or at the unfolding vistas before them. Caroline wears her honeymoon dress of deepest red, a red symbolising her love for her artist husband; her Indian shawl was a wedding gift from her uncle and aunt and though the day is bright and warm, she knows she will need it, as they climb high into the brisk air above the town. Curls fall from the clips in her hair and her rosy cheeks and sparkling eyes render her a glow that shines into Caspar's heart.

Quickly, they climb the steep path that leads out of the little town, leaving behind the bustle of the fish market and the hostelries that line the harbour. The path rises into the beech woods, winding with the contours, following the ditches between chalk banks. Up and down and up again, they rise until they are high, high above the glistening sea below. The chalk cliffs drop steeply to the shoreline, where the shallow water is so intense an emerald green, that looking at the seabed beneath the surface is as if looking through coloured glass. Columns and outcrops rise from the cliff face and from the sea bed in a multitude of forms, sculptured by the elements that hold sway on the coast of Pomerania. They have it all to themselves; they meet no other person all morning, though they are faintly aware of a man in green, in the distance far behind them.

As they reach the summit, the dappled sunlight flickers through the beeches onto their faces and they lean over the edge, speechless at the drama of the tremendous drop and the sights below and the view before them.

Caroline gazes, breathless from the climb and from the beauty of the scene before her. She says nothing, fearing disappointment, but she prays that her husband will be moved to paint a scene such as this. Caspar, silent in awe, he who knows the drama of night skies and Gothic ruins, barren landscapes and morning mists, now, for the first time, wonders if there may be something yet more wonderful in painting God's creation full of light. Like so many of his artist friends, he finds himself disillusioned nowadays with the materialist society in which they live. He regards his everyday blue coat as a symbol of his faith in a spiritual dimension, beyond the blatant attractions of clothes, carriages, expensive fabrics and furnishings. Books, music, art — now, that's the thing. Looking at the view spread out in front of him, his heart swells with a yearning to paint its glory and to capture the meaning of what he sees.

He knows he has been lucky to find Caroline. She is the daughter of a friend of his, a dyer from Dresden, who buys his dyes

180

from the merchant's house where Caspar buys his paints. In truth, she is not so very young, and she had been expecting to live out her days caring for her ageing father, having now no other known and living siblings with whom to share the role. Still, she is younger than Caspar, and he knows that he is not a handsome man, nor, being an artist, is he ever likely to have a secure income or a comfortable life. They are both happy to have found someone to care for, to be loved by, to love.

As they gaze at the scene and at the little boats sailing in the distance on the sparkling sea, they at last become aware of the figure in green behind them, leaning against the trunk of a swaying beech tree.

Caroline turns and holds out her arm, as if to share the beauty. As she does so, she gasps, for there is Johann, her much-loved and long-lost brother.

"I am back, Sister. I arrived with first light this morning, on the ferry from Bornholm, and I am here to stay." He opens his arms out wide and Caroline is wrapped into them. Caspar stands by, his hat in his hands.

At last, Caroline comes to her senses, "Johann, here is your brother-in-law, Caspar; we are just married." The two men smile warmly, and bow to each other.

Together, all three happy souls set off down the path back to the little town of Saßnitz, chattering about all that has happened in the intervening years. Johann tells how, on alighting from the ferry that very morning, after twelve years as a political prisoner on the island of Frederiksø, off Bornholm, he saw a figure that reminded him so much of his dear sister, that he was not able to resist following her. Only as he approached the couple and heard her so familiar voice, did he realise that his long-held dream had come true. The delight with which he stood patiently, waiting for her to turn, was, he says, his happiest moment since leaving home all those years ago.

The hope that Johann had, during all those years, that he would again see his sister, and the faith that Caspar had, that his wife's happiness would one day be complete, have come about. What more can anyone ask of life?

ENGLISH AS A FOREIGN LANGUAGE
LESSON 72 – PHRASAL VERBS

Avril Suddaby

Teacher: This week, Manuel, you want to learn about phrasal verbs. I'm sure you remember that a phrasal verb is a verb with a preposition added to it. Often this gives a completely new meaning to the verb. Let's begin with one which you know already – to put on.

Student: Yes, I remember. I put on my hat and scarf and coat.

Teacher: Very good, Manuel. Now what about the opposite of put on your hat and coat?

Student: I put off my hat and coat?

Teacher: No, Manuel. The opposite of put on your hat and coat is to take off your hat and coat. Put off has a different meaning.

Student: Please explain me put off.

Teacher: OK then. My mother-in-law wants to visit us next weekend. Because it's not very convenient I'd like to put off her visit until a later date.

Student: I see. Put off means to postpone.

Teacher: Exactly. Postpone is the right English word but the English love their phrasal verbs and often prefer them to a simpler more direct way of saying something.

Student: Yes, my English friend often says "I'll ring you up". For a long time I puzzled about this 'up'. I see in my EFL Dictionary there are many phrasal verbs with 'put'. A few weeks ago we put forward our clocks when we changed from Greenwich Mean Time to British Summer Time.

Teacher: Very good, Manuel, except we say we put the clocks forward. If you put something forward you propose or suggest it as a good idea. And if I put someone forward for a job it means I recommend him. You see, the position of the preposition in the sentence can alter the meaning.

Student: Next autumn will we put back the clocks or will we put the clocks back?

Teacher: We'll put the clocks back one hour. To put back the clock means to replace it. For example, if you took it off the wall to adjust the time, then you'd put it back afterwards.

Student: What about 'put in' and 'put out'?

Teacher: You put out a fire or a cigarette. You put in an application for a job which you'd like to have.

Student: And put away?

Teacher: When my mother-in-law comes to stay she always puts everything away in the wrong place in the kitchen, so that we can't find anything afterwards.

Student: And to put up and put down?

Teacher: Put up means to give someone accommodation in your home for a few days. I must put up my mother-in-law for three days next week.

Student: And what does it mean if you put down your mother-in-law?

Teacher: No, Manuel, I cannot do this to my mother-in-law. Put down is when the vet puts an animal to sleep because it is very old or ill. It means merciful killing or euthanasia.

Student: I agree. You cannot do this to your mother-in-law.

Teacher: No, I must just put up with the situation. Ah, I realise that I have just used a complicated phrasal verb which uses not just one but two prepositions. Put up with means to endure or tolerate something.

Student: Learning English as a foreign language is very difficult.

Teacher: I can assure you, Manuel, that teaching English as a foreign language is also very difficult.

Student: Let me see what I remember from today's lesson. You would like to put off your mother-in-law's visit. When she stays, she puts away everything in the wrong places in the kitchen. You prefer not to put her up next week. Maybe you'd like to put down your mother-in-law. As this isn't possible, it's a problem which you must put up with.

Teacher: Yes, that's correct, Manuel.

Student: I remember another rule about the English language. It is that you should never end a sentence with a preposition. But here–we have just ended with two prepositions: you said, it is a problem you must put up with.

Teacher: Yes, I've heard of this rule too, Manuel. But now I am very tired. Shall we put off discussing this until next lesson?

AUNTIE JANE

Moira Newlan

She had lived to a good old age, my Auntie Jane. Had outlived her other siblings, one of whom was my mother. Although we lived hundreds of miles apart and seldom saw each other, we kept in regular contact. I rang her most weeks.

I liked her very much. She was always very supportive of my less orthodox choices, unlike my own mother. I also felt slightly sorry for her, unmarried with no children of her own, and dull decades spent in the Civil Service until she retired. Her generation had not enjoyed all those opportunities which my generation had been given. She was also my god mother, and there was a special bond between us.

It had naturally befallen me to clear her house after she died. It's a dreary task, as everyone acknowledges. But the task had been made much easier as my highly organised and methodical Auntie Jane had anticipated this day, at the time when she had moved into her tiny, terraced home a few years earlier. She had told me not to worry, as she had already dealt with all her unwanted items and her large number of books before that move had taken place. *But why not move into a flat*, I had asked my Aunt. *The stairs*, she replied, *were good for my legs and the garden was good for my soul.*

We had visited her a couple of years before on our way up to Scotland for a holiday. Everything was as she had said: uncluttered, but comfortable and homely. We had indeed been spared the accumulated paraphernalia left by so many older people, stashed away in assorted containers in garages and lofts and wardrobes.

We had allowed ourselves three days to divide up items for house clearance or, as my Aunt had previously specified, *It's for the British Heart Foundation.* We had labelled any valuable items to show to an auction house, and the little which remained was bagged or taken to the local charity shop.

Auntie Jane had certainly been organised. In her appearance as well, she had taken meticulous care, with manicured nails and a flattering style for her soft grey hair. My mother had hinted that she was a bit of dark horse, whatever that meant. Apparently, she had travelled quite a lot with work, but Mum didn't know any of the details. Her sister's letters home had been chatty and full of observations about the weather or food or the museum she had visited, but contained little personal information.

I had asked why my Aunt had never married. *Never found the right man,* it seems. Though as far as Mum could gather, there had been several offers. *Married to her work, though I can't think why,* Mum had chirped. *All that dreary secretarial work in the dungeons of the Civil Service.*

After retiring, my aunt had kept herself busy with volunteer work, playing bridge and gardening. I don't know what else she did, we never really discussed her day-to-day routine.

By mid-morning on our last day, it looked as if our task had been completed. Everything had been accounted for, and a small box of sentimental items now lay in the boot of our car. As I surveyed how much, or how little cleaning we could get away with, I looked up for cobwebs and noticed the loft hatch. The loft! We'd forgotten all about that.

There won't be anything up here, I'm sure, judging by your aunt's laudable organisation so far, said George. I agreed. I also wondered how her old legs could climb the stepladder, let alone squeeze through the opening. I could hear him sneezing and treading across the floor above. Then shouting that there *was* a box there. *Not too big, coming down now. It's probably some moth-eaten clothes from decades ago. Sentimental value and all that.*

I carefully blew away the dust and opened the lid. Wrapped in layers of yellowing tissue paper, lay a black velvet cape lined with scarlet. I lifted it up, tempted to drape it round my shoulders. It was still in perfect condition. It felt so sensual and glamourous. As I folded it up again, I noticed a small pocket in the lining. *Very discreet*, I thought and wondered what she had kept in there.

Folded in tissue below the cape, lay a silk dressing gown and an enormous fur hat. Underneath lay a pile of letters, mostly tucked into those old blue aerogram envelopes, a pile of postcards wrapped up in a red ribbon, and a large manilla foolscap envelope containing old black and white photographs.

Unable to control my curiosity, I opened one of the letters. I already felt like a voyeur, for these were surely private, even in death. I recognised my aunt's neat handwriting but that was all. It was a love letter, a very explicit love letter, conveying in some details her gratification . . . I stopped reading and quickly put it back. Who would have thought . . . and why would she have had it returned? Or maybe it had never been sent?

Gingerly, I opened another one at random. It was indecipherable, not because the letters weren't clearly formed, for they were. But the letters and symbols didn't make sense. There it was again on one of the postcards. A code? I could see postcards from various cities: Paris, Amsterdam, Leipzig and, yes - Leningrad. It was hard to read them, the words broken down through time and decay. Here was a place name, a date . . . innocent enough.

I spread the photographs across the carpet. Some I recognised, much the same as the ones I had inherited. My grandparents staring out at the camera, my aunt and uncle, as adolescents, and another of them taken at a wedding. Others revealed a beautiful young woman in various stages of undress, pouting, smiling,

189

posing like a film star. My aunt, I assumed. Who took them? And there were the counterparts: various young men, some in uniform, some elegantly dressed smoking cigarettes, others barely clothed. At the very bottom of the box lay two old passports. Even with the poor quality, the image revealed a beautiful young woman with dark hair carefully gathered. Dated 1956, London. The other passport showed a similar photograph, only this time her hair was short and she wore small spectacles. The script wasn't in English either. Dated 1957, stamped 'Москва'.

Next to the passports lay a small navy velvet box. Inside was a medal, and a tightly folded typewritten letter, from the head of MI5 congratulating Auntie Jane on her important under-cover services to the Nation.

I was stunned.

This sweet old lady had not only been glamorous and promiscuous but probably a British secret agent, operating in the East during the Cold War. Perhaps it was this sudden shift in perspective, that made me look around the house with new eyes. In the dusty circle left where the wall clock had been removed, I could see a faint gleam of a metal ring. *A safe?* whispered George, who was a reader of crime fiction. We took a closer look. It was cleverly concealed, a miniscule device which surely only a few people could acquire, people with access to knowledge and power. Without the code the contents of the safe would remain secret forever.

Searching more eagerly now, we noticed two larger than normal cracks between the floorboards where the doormat had been. George bent down to investigate, edging the board to one side just enough to be able to slip his hand underneath. He shone his phone-torch into the chasm. Silently, he lifted out something quite heavy, wrapped in an oily cloth. He peeled away the layers wrapping the object to reveal a small handgun. He opened the breach, *My God Jenny, it's still loaded!*

THE RIVER
Patrick Linehan

At its widest it measured no more than six yards – a brook really – and yet we called it 'The River'. It meandered through the local farmlands, turning and twisting in deference to rises or rocks in the dimpled Irish landscape, carrying the seeds of sallow and hazel to populate its angles and glens with copses. It brought water to them, and to us.

It gave us more than water; it gave us as bathing pools, in the holes it gouged in its bed when in flood. We would disport ourselves beside these on the hottest weekend days of summer, taking time out to rag each other before jumping in, nude, elbows and knees flailing. The main aim was to make the maximum of noise while splashing our reclining comrades, especially those fully clothed, with as much water as we could displace. Most of us, the single men and boys of the parish, would not admit that we swam in the river because we bathed only in the summer, and then not often. Instead, we conspired to pass it off as a communal rite of passage and a bit of fun. 'Poolside' was a fertile ground for romance, for often the approach of giggling girls would send us shouting and running for our clothes, which we would drag on without the benefit of towelling off first. We would then recline, damp and nonchalant, to pass the time flirting.

Primitive? It didn't seem like it, even in the 'modern' 1950s.

Should more mature, respectably married ladies chance upon us while taking the air, they would avert their eyes and we would tacitly conspire with them not to notice each other until they had passed by.

The River gave our cattle water. It was, also, their refuge from the 'fly', one of the various forms of gadfly which abounded in the waters. For, at whatever hour the dead heat of the day came, the 'fly' came too. The first sign was when animals, placidly grazing in the mid-morning, suddenly started to gallop, in their efforts spurting jets of excrement, with their tails high. They ran for The River where they would stand for most of the day in the shade, swishing water with their tails at their invisible enemy.

We trotted our horses to The River in the summer-holiday dinner breaks, after mornings working in the turnip field or haymaking. They would stand, cooling their fetlocks and in their eagerness to drink gallons of water through their teeth, they would pull at the reins, giving us rope burns on our young hands. We were taught to let them waddle homewards, a glut of water sloshing around in their full bellies.

In the summer, there was drought and The River would dwindle to a rivulet, in places it appeared to have dried up entirely. Man and cattle seemed to shrivel. It took the thunderstorms of August and autumn to bring relief from the heat.

Came the harvest, came the threshing. A great belching steam engine would pull the thresher between the stacks of sheaves. A six-inch wide canvas in haste and wet sacks thrown over the open barrel tops to reduce spillage on the return journey. The cart would pull up at the side of the greedy engine and the sizzling boiler would quickly gobble up the precious liquid, in bucketsful, before the circuit recommenced.

The August and autumn flash floods sent great torrents of cascading water to rip the surface from hills and paths and roads, the resultant gruel flooding into The River's channel. Brown and swollen, it would surge over the cow parsley on the banks, chesting-out to cover the nearby flat fields and give us the nearest thing in our experience to a lake. When the water receded, it left silt and detritus to enrich the land it had covered. For our part, we replaced the stepping stones at the crossings in the shallows; they would have been rolled away, often end over end, by the strength of the flood.

In the early stages of a flood, too, the fishermen among us would tie line to pole, and hook to line, and worm to hook; then, hurriedly, as The River brought plentiful supplies downstream, we would cast our worms on the water and the trout would bite. We would go home with supper in the bag, but we had to gut the fish before the women-folk would condescend to fry them.

In the long darkening evenings of Autumn and the stormy freezing nights of Winter, we would sit, before bedtime, toasting our feet around the peat fire and terrorising each other, and ourselves, with stories of massive eels that could slither across the slushy snow of the countryside from river to river. They could pause in the graveyards to bore down to the most recently buried corpse and gorge themselves on the suppurating flesh. Which was why eels were not for consumption by decent people but for export to the French who could make a delicacy out of anything.

In November, the salmon would come to spawn, great, long, tired fish, home from the sea. The cock, large and speckled, with his big tooth in his lower jaw; the hen almost nondescript, her instincts guiding her to her native gravel-bed where she would shed her load of eggs.

To us the River was ever present, ever changing, ever supportive of the life within it and outside it. In terms of rivers, it might only have been a brook, but it punched considerably above its own width.

WHERE IS HOME?

Shirley Buxton

An owl screeched in the moonlight and Marty longed to be outside, away from the memories of the last four hours: raised voices, thumps, bumps, cries, screams, crashing furniture, angry accusations, the slamming of a door and worst of all, silence.

He peered through his bedroom window. An inviting calm lay beyond the pane. He grabbed a few belongings and stuffed them into his rucksack, swung it over his shoulder and crept downstairs. He shut his eyes to the carnage caused by the latest domestic eruption. It was 'normal' in their household, but this was the first time that he had not buried his head under the bed covers. This time was different because the slamming door was not his father stomping off to the pub, it was his mother leaving. Marty knew it was safer for him to leave too. He glanced into the hall mirror; cracked, reflecting the broken home he was leaving.

He headed to the park, away from neighbours and street lights. Locked gates were no problem for a wiry ten-year-old lad. Slinging his pack over the gates, he scrambled up the wrought iron structure and dropped down on the other side. Keeping in the shadows of the hedgerow, he made his way into the wooded thicket and to his den. He and his friend Max had found this hideaway a couple of years ago, both needing an escape from violence and abuse. Max was no longer around. Max had been sent by a court order to live with his mum's sister. How Marty missed his soul mate.

Marty slid through the opening and settled his back against the tree trunk. This could hardly be his new home. It was fine in good weather but the carefully placed branches roofed with bracken were poor protection against rain. He reached up into a hollow and extracted his provisions box, an opened packet of biscuits and a half-eaten Easter egg, not much but better than nothing. He had to make a plan. He was safe until at least mid-morning when his father would awake from his drunken stupor and then, hopefully he would think Marty had left for school as usual. The school was used to the frequent absences of a child from a dysfunctional family, so he probably wouldn't be missed until teatime. Best that he tried to snatch a couple of hours sleep.

He lay there, curled up in his coat, the trauma of the night before playing over and over in his mind. Most of the children in his class seemed to have very different home lives to him. On the odd occasion that he had been invited home by a classmate he realised how different their homes were to his own. The order and rules of school extended into their home lives. There were expectations and ways of doing things which were alien to him. Food came on plates and some families sat down to eat together. People expected that things were kept in set places. Clothes were washed, dried and folded. Other people didn't have piles of worn clothes to be scrabbled through to find something fit to wear for school each morning. It was all unfamiliar and Marty always felt rather uncomfortable and out of place. He was never invited back. How he missed Max.

It was light when he awoke. Birds were twittering and tweeting. They, like him, had been nestled in trees all night. They survived; so could he. Crunching on a couple of stale biscuits, Marty pondered his next move. He needed a new life. He wondered where his Mum was. He imagined she was with a friend, keeping well out of Dad's way. She'd be okay, she was tough.

He'd make a home somewhere. He had a feeling that what was referred to as 'home' was just a place, in his experience, a rather unpleasant place. What he needed was a space which he could own and be safe, free from fear and uncertainty. Grown-ups were trouble in his experience. They only cared about themselves. Parents were too absorbed in their own problems, neighbours didn't want to be involved with problem families and teachers were obsessed with learning and results.

He wondered where Max was and if he was happy. What had he overheard when Max went away? Something about sea-air, and a place name that he'd not known but he had a vague memory that it was near Lowestoft. What he needed was a map. Perhaps if he could see the names he might be able to pick it out. There might be something at the bus station. He had his bus pass. He'd have to use that to get away from here so he wouldn't be found. To go where he would have a chance of meeting up with Max would be a bonus. Marty had his plan: get away from here; get to Lowestoft; find Max.

ABOUT EX-CATHEDRA, Norwich

Ex-Cathedra is a keen and close-knit writing group of seven members, which developed from a creative writing course studied at Norwich Cathedral in 2008 and 2009. Only three of those original seven members remain in the group, though it continues to flourish and to attract new writers.

Members of the group find that sharing and critiquing one another's work is both stimulating and enjoyable, adding to the pleasure they already get from their writing.

Ex-Cathedra has published two previous anthologies, *Voices from the Cathedral* (2010), and *Ten Minute Tales* (2017). The latter was published to raise funds for the Alzheimer's Society in Norwich, and the stories and poems which were included were deliberately short and intended to provoke memories in those who either heard them read, or were able to read them themselves.

Our decision to donate the profits from sales of this book to St Martins Housing Trust came from witnessing the very high levels of housing need in and around Norwich, and our awareness of how lucky we were to have safe homes when so many people, through no choice of their own, have none. We very much hope that sales of this book will raise much needed funds to help St Martins Housing Trust's valuable work to help the homeless into independent living.

The Writers of Ex-Cathedra are -

Shirley Buxton is one of the longest standing members of Ex-Cathedra. Her interest in writing developed in the period following her retirement from teaching. She draws inspiration from her past experiences, travel, her grandchildren and the life and writings of the fourteenth century mystic, Julian of Norwich.

Alison Court has, all her life, written journals of her travels, from Shingle Street (Suffolk) when she was nine, to Ulan Bator (Mongolia) some decades later. It was only five years ago, when she settled in Norwich, City of Literature, that she at last started to write the stories she had thought of for so long. The activities that had diverted her all those years were such as singing with friends in a chamber choir, sewing for craft fairs, walking her beloved golden retriever, reading women's literature of the 19th and 20th centuries and, above all else, hanging out with her husband and son.

Patrick Linehan was born in Southern Ireland. Books and sources of the written word were sparse, and radio also almost non-existent in Irish farming circles at that time. On completion of secondary education, he moved to London where he had a variety of jobs, including 'Nippy' (waiter in a Lyons Teashop) which gave him a feel for the city and its denizens. After about 2 years, he was fortunate enough to be accepted for the Civil Service where he spent almost 20 years. He retired to play golf and to fit in travel in Ireland, England and Europe. He lives near Norwich, with his caring and beloved wife, Moira.

Stuart McCarthy is a twice-retired writer and storyteller. He retired from teaching after thirty years working in Essex and

Norfolk primary schools. He later retired again, from a career in retail to act as a full-time carer. Writing is his greatest pleasure although he is also an accomplished 'stand up' storyteller.

Moira Newlan worked for many years in Arts Administration and in Art History Education - in both Colleges and in a National Art Gallery. She has also worked as an Alternative Therapist for over 30 years. She moved from London to Norwich five years ago, and thoroughly enjoys the creative life of this beautiful city.

Avril Suddaby came to Norwich, city of stories, 15 years ago. She soon became a member of Ex Cathedra, and with the aid and inspiration of her colleagues in this creative writing group, she began to make her own modest contribution to the literature of this fine city. Avril has been a teacher for most of her working life. She is married and has two children and four grandchildren.

Nicola L C Talbot is a chartered mathematician with a PhD in electronic systems engineering and a diploma in creative writing. After a stint as a production editor for the Challenges in Machine Learning group, she set up Dickimaw Books to publish her text books and fiction. She grew up in Sussex but has lived in the Norfolk village of Saxlingham Nethergate for twenty years with her husband and son and, before that, for ten years in Norwich.